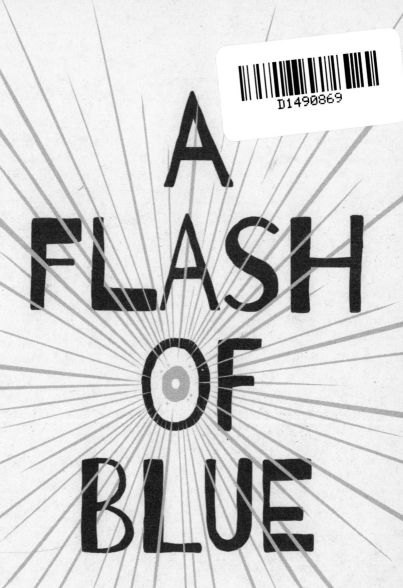

A
FLASH
OF
BLUE

SCHOLASTIC

A FLASH OF BLUE

Maria Farrer

First published in the UK in 2015 by Scholastic Children's Books
An imprint of Scholastic Ltd
Euston House, 24 Eversholt Street
London, NW1 1DB, UK

Registered office: Westfield Road, Southam, Warwickshire, CV47 0RA
SCHOLASTIC and associated logos are trademarks and/
or registered trademarks of Scholastic Inc.

ISBN 978 1407 13817 6

A CIP catalogue record for this book
is available from the British Library.

Printed by CPI Group (UK) Ltd, Croydon, CR0 4YY
Papers used by Scholastic Children's Books
are made from wood grown in sustainable forests.

1 3 5 7 9 10 8 6 4 2

www.scholastic.co.uk

For Max

♥

PROLOGUE

27th June

It started with a text from Kelly.

I can't believe it about Liam. It's so awful. Call me.

That really upsets me. Liam's my brother and if he's told Kelly something before telling me, I'll never forgive him. I try calling Kelly, but there's no answer.

Then I text Liam:

What's going on Bro? What have you told Kelly?

My boss is frowning at me. Phones are supposed to be off when we're on duty. I smile an apology and slip my phone back into my pocket, then go and take the order from table three.

I doubt I'll get an answer from Liam. He'll make me sweat it out. We argued – again – last night. I only wanted to borrow his phone charger, but the way he kicked off, you'd have thought World War Three had broken out. That's how it is between Liam and me these days. Fair enough, it was my stupid fault for losing my own charger, but there's no need to overreact. Just because he and his best mate Tyler were in the middle of some manic PlayStation battle and couldn't be bothered to open the bedroom door. If Liam hadn't started locking his door all the time, I could have gone in, helped myself to his charger and saved us both the hassle. Instead, I got shouted at by Liam and then by Mum, who told me to leave Liam alone and to learn to look after my things. Later I heard Liam and Tyler arguing and one of them must've chucked the charger out the door because it was lying in the corridor. Why didn't they do that in the first place?

Liam and me have always been close. That's what makes this so hard. All of a sudden I can nothing right. Even though it's fifty/fifty Liam and me starting the arguments, it's always me who gets the blame – ALWAYS. Somehow Liam's bad mood has become *my* fault. Dad says I must respect the fact that Liam is now an adult. So you turn eighteen and you change overnight? Stuff that. If becoming an adult means turning into a self-centred, uncommunicative, over-aggressive moron, then kill me now. Which, come to think of it, is probably what Liam is planning to do. . .

. . .because this morning. OK, this morning maybe I crossed the line. I stole Liam's stone. It was a spur of the moment thing. Opportunistic. He only ever takes it off when he's in the shower and this morning, when I went in after him, he'd left it hanging on the back of the bathroom door. He's dead superstitious about his lucky stone and I've never seen him leave the house without it. The trouble is, this morning I left the house first – with it. I didn't really have a plan beyond getting him to communicate with me. I don't want to carry on like we are at the moment; I hate it. So I'm counting on him being so desperate to get it back that he'll have no option but to talk. And you know what? It seems my plan has worked. As soon as he realized it was missing, he phoned all of us in panic. I wasn't going to lie to him. He went crazy at first, but I told him if he wanted his stone, he was going to have to listen to me. He put the phone down. A few minutes later he rang back.

"You're right," he said. "We do need to talk. Not on the phone. There's something I've been meaning to tell you and I'd rather do it face-to-face. Meet outside the library after work?"

I asked him if he was OK and he said he was fine. But he didn't sound fine.

I finger Liam's stone around my neck, then check my boss, Cathy, isn't looking before reading Kelly's text again. What would Kelly find so hard to believe about Liam? I don't want to be the last person to know. What could be so awful? And why would he tell Kelly? She's my friend, not his. And then I start to worry.

So when a policeman strides into the café, just after the lunchtime rush is over, some illogical instinct tells me it has something to do with Liam. My first thought is that he has decided to get revenge and has actually reported me to the police for nicking his stone. But that's just stupid. I tell myself that a policeman could be here for any reason – I mean, maybe he just wants a cup of coffee. I decide to stay out of sight in the kitchen. And then I start to wonder . . . what if Liam really is in trouble – like, serious trouble – with the law? I shake my head. Liam's not like that.

I strain to hear what the policeman is saying as he talks to Simon, who works at the café with me. I watch Simon nod and turn towards the kitchen door. Why is my heart beating so fast?

"He wants to know where your mum is," Simon whispers to me.

"Mum? She's in London. Why's he asking?" Now I start worrying about Mum.

"The police want to talk to her."

"To Mum? What do the police want with Mum?"

Simon spreads his hands and turns down the corners of his mouth. "You'd better come out."

I wipe my hands quickly. When I appear, the policeman indicates a recently vacated table and asks if we can sit. I nod. There's a sense of purposeful urgency to his movements.

"Are you Amber Neville?"

"Yes."

"And this is your mum's café?"

"Yes. Why?"

He smiles gently. "I'm PC Marsh." He flashes me his ID. "I need to speak to her."

"She's in London. Is it important?" His mixture of niceness and directness is making me nervous.

"Yes, I'm afraid it is."

5

"I can give you her mobile number." I fumble for my phone.

"We've tried that but there's no answer."

I let my phone drop to my side. "She might have her phone switched off. She's visiting a friend in hospital." I give him a few details and he jots them down.

"That's very helpful. Thank you. Excuse me one moment. I'll be back." He walks towards the door.

I feel both confused and relieved.

"What's going on?" asks Simon.

"No idea." I check my phone again. No new messages. I scroll back to Kelly's text and the knot of uneasiness builds in my stomach. I try ringing her again, and Liam, and Mum.

Nothing.

"Is everything OK?" Cathy asks. I shrug. I have no idea.

There are a few orders left on the serving hatch ready to go out. Customers are waiting. Having a policeman hovering around the café has made people watchful and uncomfortable. PC Marsh is outside the café window, chin dipped towards his collar as he talks into a mouthpiece. Police don't turn up asking questions for nothing. I try to smile and carry on business as usual, taking orders, clearing tables, but

6

my eyes keep flicking to what is happening outside. Then, out of the corner of my eye, I see the familiar figure of Gran rushing towards the café. Except it isn't familiar. Gran often helps out at the café in the afternoons, but she never rushes because of her dodgy heart. Now she's almost running.

I put down my tray and go to the door, holding it open for her.

"Gran?"

I already know, before she opens her mouth, that something is very wrong. She staggers the last few steps towards the nearest table and leans on it heavily, her hand hovering over her chest.

"Are you all right?" I pull a chair round behind her and help her sit down.

"No . . . not really . . . my pills." She pushes her bag towards me and I scrabble through it. It takes me a few moments to find her small blue box. I hand her one of the tiny pills and she slips it under her tongue.

At the same time, PC Marsh walks back in and joins us. Everyone's eyes are on us now.

"Mrs Turner?" He asks Gran.

She gives him a weak smile and a nod.

"Good, I'm glad you're here. I think I'd better

get you to the hospital as quickly as possible."

"It's all right," I say. "I've given her one of her pills already."

PC Marsh shakes his head.

"It's Liam," Gran says, taking my hand. "He's had an accident."

The café mists over, vision and sound suddenly grey and indistinct. I watch in slow motion as the policeman moves forward to help Gran up from her chair.

"I'll need another moment," she says, "to get my breath back."

And everything rushes back to full speed, full clarity. "What kind of an accident?" I ask, my voice almost unrecognizable to my own ears.

Gran doesn't quite meet my eyes. "He collapsed during training."

I laugh. This is some mistake. They've got the wrong person. "Don't be silly, Liam's one of the fittest people I know."

Gran glances at the policeman and then covers her mouth with her hand. I'll never forget that look.

"Your brother is in intensive care," says PC Marsh gently. "He has a friend with him and your mum is on her way home. We haven't managed to get hold of your dad yet. I'm going to take you and your grandmother to the hospital."

Intensive care? A friend? My hand slips between the buttons of my shirt and my fingers close around Liam's stone. I have to get to the hospital as fast as possible. I have to give him his lucky stone back. I should never have taken it. We need to leave *now*. If necessary, I'll pick Gran up and carry her. I don't bother to get my bag. I don't stop to explain to Cathy or Simon.

I link my arm through Gran's as we walk towards the car park, trying to hurry her along. I so badly want to run, but we have to go at her speed and it feels agonizingly slow. There's not one calm cell in my body and my mind is on overtime. I need to know exactly what's happened. I need Liam to tell me everything. I need to be there with him right now.

I'd always thought riding in a police car would be exciting, but not like this. We drive quickly, but not quickly enough, and each time we come up against any traffic, the blue lights flash and we whizz on through. I grip the stone. I know that as soon as I give it back to Liam everything will be all right.

My phone buzzes and my heart stops for a couple

of beats. I will it to be Liam. He'll tell me he's fine. He'll say we can all stop worrying. That's what he always does – when he comes back from one of his long training runs or something.

"I'd leave that if I were you," says Gran.

"But what if it's Liam?"

"He's in intensive care, Amber. He won't be using his phone." She prises the phone from my fingers. "Why don't you let me look after it for you, sweetheart?" she says, putting it in her handbag.

Liam is dead by the time we get to the hospital. Apparently he never regained consciousness. His best friend Tyler was with him.

I was too late.

CHAPTER 1

Almost a year later...

The sky is so dark it could be night; not the towering clouds of a storm but the flat, dark grey that has more water in it than the sea. I up my pace and feel my pulse surge in response. I'll never get back before the rain, however fast I run. I'm still forty minutes from home.

The first thick, fat drops fall on my face, mixing with sweat and sending salty rivers dribbling from my forehead into my eyes. I wipe them away. The final steep hill is approaching and after that it's a gentle 5k back to our house. My body angles forwards slightly as I begin the climb. Immediately, I feel the dull pain just below my left kneecap. It's been bugging me recently, but I try not to mention it. Dad doesn't do complaining.

My breath comes short and loud and I swear as I hit the steepest pinch of the hill. The rain hammers down, bouncing off the road and turning the pale blue of my shirt uniformly darker, the material clinging to my body.

At the crest of the hill, I know I mustn't decelerate. I extend my stride and pump my arms. A car passes, its lights cutting through the grey, its tyres sending up great fans of water. I yell after it, but it makes no difference. I couldn't get any wetter if I tried.

The houses on our road are coming to life; people are getting up for breakfast. It's 8.30 on a Saturday morning and I've already completed 15k — or will have done by the time I reach my front door. Dad's measured out all my runs. Saturday's is always a long one.

Relief sets in as I squelch back up our short path and slump forward with my finger on the doorbell. I rest my hands on my knees and watch the water dripping off my hair and the faint steam rising from my body.

The shape of my father looms behind the frosted glass of the door. He opens it and holds out the stopwatch.

"Not your best time," he says.

I gesture aggressively at the sky as if to say, *Well, who's going to do a good time in conditions like this?*

"Over four minutes off your personal best – you won't win the race with that kind of time."

I lean against the door frame and listen to my heart beating. I went through extensive tests after Liam died. My heart is fine, apparently. I have no excuse not to run. No excuse not to win. The cold from my saturated clothes seeps into my skin and through my body. I thought it was supposed to be June. It's more like mid-winter.

"Are you going to let me in? My muscles are seizing up out here."

Dad stands aside. I put a foot over the door and he puts his hand on my shoulder and holds me back.

"Shoes off!" He stares at my soggy trainers. "You're not bringing those in here."

I try to pull them off without undoing the laces but it's as if they're attached with suction pads. I have to sit on the doorstep and wrench them from my feet before peeling off my socks and wringing them out.

Finally, Dad lets me in, closes the door on the rain and throws a towel at me. I put it over my head, rub down my hair, then shift the towel to my shoulders for warmth. I head straight towards the bathroom for a shower.

"Come back and have a drink," shouts Dad, stopping me in my tracks. "You don't realize how much you sweat when it's wet." He's sitting at the kitchen table, frowning as he records my time on his laptop.

"You don't know how cold I get when it's wet," I mumble. He watches as I pour a glass of water and gulp it down and then he gives me a nod to show he's done with me. I force my legs up the stairs and into the bathroom, locking the door behind me. For a few seconds, I lean against it, too tired to move. Then I switch on the shower, undress and wait for the water to warm up. I try not to look at myself in the mirror. I hate my reflection – my body hard, lean and muscled and my hair cropped short. I'm growing to look more and more like my brother and it seems unfair.

The heat of the water shocks my skin, turning it blotchy and red. As I readjust to the temperature, I keep turning it hotter and hotter, letting the warmth sink in. I scrub off the mud, stretch each set of muscles and massage the tenderness below my knee. I could stay in here all morning, eyes closed, hot water raining down on the back of my neck.

Liam made Dad put in a good shower last year. He said he wasn't doing all this training and coming home to a pathetic dribble. I can't get into the shower without thinking of Liam. I can't do anything without thinking of Liam.

Sometimes I talk to him in my head. I like to believe he can hear me. I like to think it will make a difference. Sometimes I smile. Usually I cry. Mostly I'm swamped with guilt.

Someone told me it would get easier, but it's been nearly a year now. Each day, each hour brings us closer to the anniversary of Liam's death. No one talks about it. It's just there, looming ahead of us like a huge black hole, sucking us slowly towards it.

As the days pass, it does not get easier. It gets stronger and more dangerous.

CHAPTER 2

It's just a stone.

I sit on my bed, wrapped in my towel, staring at Liam's stone in my hand.

We found it when we were on holiday in Dorset; it must be almost ten years ago now. Liam was nine and me six. Mum and Dad had rented a caravan and we spent every day on the beach near Durdle Door. I loved that name – Durdle Door. Dad always said it in funny ways to make us laugh. *Durdly, dawdly, diddly door. Diddly, widdly, piddly door.* That one always cracked me up. I only remember snippets: Liam teaching me to how to skim pebbles across the flat calm sea; Dad digging an enormous racing car out of sand; Mum decorating it with shells. We used a stick for the gear lever and we played in it for hours. We went back the next day and it was gone –

washed away by the tide. I was heartbroken. Mum swinging me round and round by the arms to make me feel better – me laughing – tottering off down the beach, dizzy as a drunk with Liam running after me and making me crawl along with him to search for fossils.

That's when we found the stone – when *he* found the stone.

It was perfectly oval in shape, washed smooth by the sea, with a small round hole straight through the centre. It wasn't much bigger than a penny and when it was wet, it shimmered blue as the water. Liam dipped it in the sea and held it up to the sky so we could see the colour and the sun shining through the hole. He told me a stone with a hole was the luckiest thing you could find. He said it was going to be his secret stone and that I mustn't tell anyone or the luck would run away. He made me promise. I thought we should share the stone, but he wouldn't let me, however much I begged. He danced around with it held high above his head, chanting, "Finders keepers".

It wasn't fair. I wanted a lucky stone too.

"Finders keepers, losers weepers," he chanted and chanted until he made me cry.

Then he took pity on me and found me a lucky shell instead, but it wasn't the same. I lost it before we got home from holiday. Not Liam — he never lost that stone. It became somehow a part of him and I really believed it brought him luck. He passed every exam with an A, won every race, made Mum and Dad proud. I lost count of the times I asked to borrow it. His reply was always the same: a small shrug and those words, "finders keepers".

I cup the stone in my hands. If I'd hoped that some of the luck would rub off on me, then I've been disappointed so far. I haven't told anyone that I've got it. Imagine what they'd say if they knew I'd taken it on the day he died? No one can ever know — not ever. I should've buried it with him, but I couldn't bring myself to let it go. I kiss it and return it to its hiding place. I raise my towel to my face, pressing hard on my eyes, pushing back the memories.

My phone pings, a welcome diversion. It's Simon. I'm supposed to have decided what film we're going to see this afternoon.

Will pick you up around 2.

Dad calls, "Amber. What are you doing up there?"

I throw on some clothes and walk gingerly down

the stairs to the kitchen. My knee is hurting and the idea of breakfast turns my stomach.

Dad's got a saucepan in one hand and a print-out of my running times in the other. "Where do you think you lost time this morning, Amber? Was it the hills? I knew we should've done more hill work. How do you want your eggs today? Fried?"

"I don't feel like eggs."

"You have to have eggs today. It's Saturday. 'Eggs any way'," he reads off the diet chart pinned to the fridge door.

"I'm having cereal. I'll have eggs tomorrow." I reach for the cornflakes.

"What is the point in me doing all this for you if you don't follow it?" He waves his hand at the chart. "Your brother always—"

"OK, Dad." I press my fingers into my temples. "I'll have eggs. Scrambled."

"Good. Go and ask your mum if she wants breakfast. Here, you can take her some coffee."

I hesitate. Their bedroom is not a good place to be in the morning, but Dad nods impatiently in the direction of the stairs, a clear order for me to go. I drag myself up and knock quietly on the door. There's no answer. I open the door little by little, trying not to make a noise. The curtains are still closed and the air smells stale – a toxic mix of alcohol and other things I'd rather not think about. The rain hasn't let up and it spatters on the windowpanes.

I go round to Mum's side of the bed and put the mug of coffee on her side table. I think of all the Sunday mornings when I used to take her coffee and sit with her in bed while Liam was training with Dad. We'd giggle about nothing in particular and make fun of Liam's obsessive running regime. Now it's me doing the running and Mum's days and nights pass in an alcoholic haze. I lean down towards her, trying not to inhale the fumes from her breath. She won't want scrambled eggs.

"Mum?" I stroke her shoulder gently and she grunts.

"What time is it?" she mumbles. "It's still dark."

"Only because the curtains are closed. Dad says do you want breakfast?"

She frowns and wrinkles her nose then rolls away from me, shaking my hand from her shoulder and pulling the duvet tightly around her.

"I've brought you coffee."

She doesn't move or make a sound.

"Mum?"

Nothing.

"Suit yourself," I mumble to the lump under the duvet. I creep towards the door and start pulling it closed as quietly as I can. I'd rather she stayed asleep when she's like this. Dad likes to pretend there's nothing wrong. Gran says he's put Mum's drinking problems in the *too-hard basket*. Most stuff belongs in the too-hard basket these days.

"Amber?" The door is nearly shut when she calls my name in a pathetic kind of wail. I sigh and step back into the room. Mum is struggling to hold her head off the pillow.

"You'll have to go over to Gran's this afternoon. I promised I'd help her with cakes for the lifeboats but I think I've got flu or something." Her head drops back on to her pillow.

Flu? Does she think I'm stupid?

"I'm going out with Simon this afternoon."

"What day is it?" She sounds tearful, confused.

"It's Saturday, Mum. You know it is. You've just told me about going to Gran's to bake cakes."

"Simon can cope on his own in the café."

"He's not working today, we're going to. . ." I

give up. It's not worth it.

"You must go to Gran's. I promised." She sounds like a frightened child.

I'd like to tell her that it's her problem and if she hadn't drunk herself senseless last night then she wouldn't have "flu" this morning and then she could keep her promise. I'd like to tell her I've promised Simon I'd go to the cinema. I can't let him down again. Then I think of poor Gran, who's always here helping out and I know I should go and help her in return.

I walk back into the kitchen. "No eggs for Mum," I say.

Dad presses his lips together and carefully puts two eggs back in the box.

I pick up my phone to text Simon. What can I say? I've stood him up so many times already and it's getting worse than embarrassing.

Can't make it today. REALLY sorry. Have to help Gran.

I press send. Dammit.

Dad and I eat breakfast in silence, then I take the plates to the dishwasher.

"Why are you limping?" he asks.

"Nothing. Just my knee. It's stiffened up a bit."

"Didn't you ice it when you got back?"

I shake my head.

"How many times do I have to tell you?" He strides to the freezer, flings open the door and grabs an ice pack. "Now sit down and get this on your leg." I go through to the living room and put myself on the sofa. Dad wraps the ice pack in a dishcloth then tapes it round my leg. "You've got to be fit for tomorrow."

Tomorrow. The running club half marathon – the final long-distance race of the season. It's not such a big deal – more for fun than anything else – but it was the last race that Liam won and it's the last trophy left in the cabinet. All the others have been handed back, the silver gleaming after Dad's cleaned them for hours, polishing and polishing over Liam's name until it was a wonder he didn't rub it out altogether. I'm not old enough to run the half marathon, but there's a 10k race for my age-group and I'm hoping to win the girls' category. If I don't, the cabinet will be empty. A trophy in the cabinet means a lot to Dad.

The blackness rolls in and there's nothing I can do to hold it back.

Why can't Dad see that I can't *be* Liam? Why

can't he see how hard it is for me even to turn up at these events? I don't know how Dad can stand it. All the old familiar crowd: people who a year ago would have loved to have seen the back of my brother so that their own precious sons would have a chance of winning. They're all respectful of Dad. Liam will always be a winner; no one can ever beat him now. That's what they tell him. Why can't Dad be content to bask in Liam's eternal triumph instead of forcing me to let him down time after time? I'm not bad at running, but I'm not a champion either. Each time I lose it hurts a little more. My friends from the club tread on eggshells around me, as if they don't know what to say or how to act. It's easier for people not to spend time with me, easier for them not to try. I'm on the fringe of every circle: standing there but invisible. Perhaps they only ever liked me because of Liam. Perhaps I'm not worth knowing any more.

I shift my leg. The ice has turned it numb. I can hear Dad clattering around in the kitchen, clearing up with barely disguised aggression. I remove the ice, drop it on the floor and let my eyes close.

The sound of the doorbell drags me back to consciousness. Dad grunts as he gets up off his chair.

I hear him open the door.

"It's for you," he says, with total lack of interest as he follows Simon into the living room.

"I was passing," Simon says. "Thought I'd pop in to see if you were OK. Sorry – did I wake you up?"

I smile, self-conscious. "Passing on your way to. . ."

"Nowhere," he laughs. "And don't worry, I'd be asleep too if I had to get up at crack of dawn to run." He looks at the ice pack on the floor. "I'm guessing you were out on this beautiful morning?"

I nod and glance at Dad. Dad gives me a stare, picks up the ice and takes it away, leaving us alone.

Sometimes I think Simon knows me better than I know myself. We've been friends since primary, though we're not at the same school any more. I move my legs off the sofa so he can sit down.

He doesn't. "It's stopped raining," he says. "Fancy a walk?"

"Are you joking?"

"Yes," he says. He takes off his jacket and plonks himself down beside me. Our knees just touch. "It's the big race tomorrow, isn't it?"

I nod.

"You shouldn't let it get you down," he says quietly. "You don't have to do it, you know."

I put my finger to my lips, sliding my eyes towards the door in case Dad can hear. Simon knows how much I hate racing. "I'll be OK."

"You'll be better if you come to the movies this afternoon."

"I can't. Gran needs help with making cakes for the lifeboats."

Simon sighs and looks down at his hands. "You don't have to make excuses. If you don't want to come you can just tell me."

"I'm not making excuses. Mum was going to help Gran but she's not well."

"Again?" he says and I think I see him roll his eyes.

I've lost count of the times I've blamed things on Mum being unwell. I'm not surprised it's wearing a bit thin.

"You're allowed a life too," he says.

Am I? I wonder.

Simon puts his hand on my arm and shakes it gently. "Hey, come on. How about we go to the cinema later then? In the evening? It'll be fun and it'll help take your mind off things."

He holds my eyes for a bit longer than feels

comfortable. A blush creeps into my cheeks.

"OK," I say. "I'll meet you in town."

"No ducking out at the last minute?" He stands up and heads for the door. "And you can bring me some cake."

"To prove I'm not lying?"

"No – because I like cake."

I can't help smiling.

"That's better," he says.

I don't want Simon to go. Sometimes it feels like he's the only person, apart from Gran, who won't give up on me.

CHAPTER 3

The sight of Gran's door is always comforting. I take extra care not to step on the grass in-between the eight paving slabs leading up to it. When we were young, Granddad told us a bear would eat us if we stepped on the grass. I always made Liam give me a piggyback.

I ring the doorbell and wait. It takes her a while to answer.

Her face breaks into a huge smile when she sees me. "This is a nice surprise. I won't hug you or I'll cover you in flour."

She's wearing her favourite apron, dusted in white. On the front, it says: "*Women are like wine, they improve with age.*" Granddad gave it to her for their fortieth anniversary.

She lets me in, peering towards the road — looking for Mum, I assume.

"I got the bus," I say. "Mum's having a bad day. She said you needed help. . ."

"She said *I* needed help?" Gran interrupts, makes a funny *what's that all about* face, but her eyes darken for a moment – just long enough for me to notice – before she snaps back to her cheerful self.

". . .with the cakes," I say, to make sure there's no misunderstanding.

"That's very kind, sweetheart, but I'm sure you've got things you'd rather be doing?"

I limp through to the kitchen where Gran's cat weaves itself in and out of my legs.

"That knee of yours is getting worse. I hope you didn't run this morning?"

"Yes. Worse luck. 15k."

"In all that rain? Shouldn't you be resting it instead of training so hard?"

I should be resting before a race day whatever, I think to myself. Dad should know that, but he's too obsessed by his training schedules.

I shrug. "Dad says it's what I have to do if I want to win."

Gran sighs a loud sigh. "And do you," she asks carefully, "want to win?"

She hands me an apron and I put it over my head

and tie it around my waist. She shoos the cat out of the kitchen.

"I would like to win. Just once. For Dad. Maybe it would help him and Mum — you know, with next weekend and everything."

Gran stops what she's doing and looks at me. I've said it now.

"Has your dad talked to you about next weekend?" she asks.

"No one talks about it." My body suddenly feels heavy and I have to lean against the side. "It's as if talking about it will make it too real. But June the 27th is always going to be the day Liam died, isn't it? We can't hide from it."

"No we can't." Gran puffs out air through her nose and her mouth is set in a grim line. She gives a quick shake of the head. "And I suppose Dad hasn't told you that he and Mum are going away?"

"Are they?" I try to process this information. "What about me?"

The words hang in the air.

"I think the plan is for you to stay here with me." Gran tries to make it sound jolly.

Tears melt into my eyes. I concentrate on opening a new bag of sugar. I've been trying so hard. How could Mum and Dad think it was OK to go away and leave me next weekend? Surely we should all be together on the day Liam died? It's not that I don't want to stay with Gran. In fact I'd rather stay with her. It's just the fact that they are doing it – that they didn't even ask me or talk to me or anything.

"We'll plan something nice," says Gran. "What would you like to do?"

But the tears are streaming down my face. Gran forgets about the flour and wraps her arms around me. "I know," she says, rocking me back and forth. "I know."

But she doesn't know. No one knows.

And now I have to face the day alone.

○

By the time I get home, it's four o'clock.

Dad's still at the kitchen table and I wonder if he's moved since I left.

Mum's made it downstairs and is curled up on the sofa with a magazine in her hand. My anger hovers dangerously close to the surface.

"Where have you been?" Mum says, looking up with a small smile when I come in.

"Helping Gran – like you told me." I try to smile back.

"Oh, yes." She goes back to her magazine.

"Thank you, Amber, for doing that for me," I supply on her behalf. She looks up at me, frowning, and I turn and run upstairs before I say something I might regret.

I don't bother to change. It's only Simon. I check my bag for money and grab my phone. I'm going to be late if I don't get a move on.

I trot back down, glad that my knee has eased.

"Where are you going?" asks Dad.

"To the cinema."

"What about the race tomorrow?"

"I had to cancel Simon this afternoon, so I thought it would be OK to go this evening instead."

"Well, it is not OK," he says.

"I'm only going to the movies!"

Dad gets out of his chair. This is a bad sign. "It's time you got your priorities sorted. You can go to the cinema any time. You need an early night."

"It's not going to be late."

"It is not going to *be*. Full stop."

I rub my eyes, hoping I might wake up from this stupid scene. "I can't let Simon down again," I beg.

"Surely it won't hurt her to. . ." Mum's come through to the kitchen and I guess she's feeling guilty about earlier.

"You'd never have seen Liam going out and messing around with girls the night before a race." Dad directs this comment at both of us and it has the desired effect on Mum. She retreats back to the living room.

"I'm not messing around with anyone. I'm going to watch a film." I grab my coat.

Dad puts himself between me and the door.

"You will do as you are told. You didn't ask our permission to go out this evening and we are not giving it."

"Well, you haven't asked my permission to go away next weekend."

That shuts him up for a second or two and I wait for the explosion. It doesn't come.

"Oh – so Gran told you, did she?" says Dad. "I might have guessed, the interfering old busybody. I was going to talk to you about it this evening."

"Were you?"

He seems confused, as if he knows he's been caught out. He puts his hands on his hips. "Anyway, it makes no difference, you are not going out tonight and that's that."

"Fine!" I know I've lost, but I can't stop. "If you don't want me to have a life, if you don't want me to have any friends, fine. But don't expect me to do all *your* dirty work for you from now on."

Dad knows what I mean. He's been going away more and more on business trips — each trip getting a little longer. I'm left to sort out Mum. She's always worse when he's away and it's a vicious circle — the worse she gets, the more he's away. And now I can hear her crying and Dad has his hands behind his head and half over his ears. I turn my back on him, stomp back up to my room, slam my door and put my ear against it to see if he's following. He isn't. I take a deep breath, kick the door and ring Simon.

"Hey, Simon, it's me."

"Hey, me. Don't tell me . . . you're running late."

"Worse. Dad's grounded me before the race tomorrow."

I hear muffled swearing, as if he's put his hand over the mouthpiece.

"That's great," he says into the phone, his voice sarcastic. "Bloody typical."

"You know how he is."

"Yeah." There's a short silence.

"I'm sorry."

In the pause that follows, I imagine Simon at the other end of the phone.

"Hey, look, never mind. We'll go another time." I can hear the flat disappointment in his voice.

"Maybe once the next week or so is over?" I say. "Things might be easier then."

"Yep."

"See you on Tuesday then? At the café?"

"OK. Bye."

"Aren't you going to wish me luck for tomorrow?"

But the phone's gone dead. I stare at it then thump it on to the bed. It's times like these that I wish, beyond anything, that Liam was still alive – the nice Liam. The Liam where I could still fling open his bedroom door, in true drama-queen fashion, and rave about the injustices of my life and he'd sit there, watching, until I'd got it all out of my system. And then he'd make me laugh and laugh until the world was right again. Oh, God. I lean forward as thoughts jumble in my head. I fold my arms across my stomach, trying to squeeze away the pain. Grief hurts. Sometimes I love Liam so much that I think my heart will burst and sometimes I burn up with anger for the mess he's left me in. Either way, whether I want to hug him or beat him up, he's not there.

Either way, I miss him.

Either way it would be better if it was me who was dead.

CHAPTER 4

The race is over. I stare out of the car window as Dad and I drive home in a silence as empty as the trophy cabinet. I've said sorry about a hundred times. I actually came close to winning and that makes it worse. I was beaten in the last 200 metres, overtaken by four people in the final sprint. Dad refused to stay for the prize-giving.

My phone pings and Dad glares at it. It's the first time he's shown any awareness that I'm in the car with him. It's an unknown number.

Party at my place on Saturday. BYO sleeping bag and drink. Bring friend if u want. X Kelly

Kelly? I frown at my phone. Saturday? Is this some kind of sick joke? She must remember what day Saturday is. I haven't heard from Kelly in ages. I think she only played at being my friend because she fancied Liam. Why else would she dump me like a hot potato when he died?

I look at the text again. Perhaps I'm being unfair. It wasn't quite as simple as that – nowhere near as simple, in fact. This time last year, Kelly's older brother, Tyler, shared the podium with Liam at prize-giving. Silver and gold in the half marathon. Liam won by less than a metre. They were best mates, even though Tyler was in the year below. They were forever training together, pushing each other further and faster. The rest of the time they'd lock themselves in Liam's room, playing music or gaming, the volume turned up so loud that they were oblivious to everything and everyone else. I hated the way they locked me out.

It was Tyler who was with Liam when he died.

I've never seen Dad lose it like he did that day at the hospital. He was screaming – screaming at the doctors and screaming at Tyler – forcing him to go over and over what happened. Dad wouldn't accept that Liam had simply collapsed. There was a huge scene, Gran and Mum trying to calm him down, doctors, nurses. And Tyler, white with shock.

"If you did anything," Dad kept saying to Tyler. "Anything. . ."

I should've stuck up for Tyler. I knew he wasn't to blame. Liam had suffered massive heart failure. It was very rare and very unlucky. That's the word they kept using, "unlucky". The shame and guilt of it engulfs me all over again.

I glance at Dad as he drives, his mouth slack, his smile muscles out of practice. Liam is dead and now Dad's left with me – a useless reminder every day of what he's lost.

Dad told everyone that it was Tyler Dawson's fault. Tyler was a bad influence. Why were he and Liam such good friends anyway? Why hadn't he come to the funeral? Dad took that as a sign of Tyler's guilt. Dad said he'd always known the Dawsons were trouble.

I didn't hear from Kelly again and, not long after, the Dawsons moved away. Rumours spread and people started to talk: Tyler and Liam had been seen bunking off school, Kelly was pregnant and Liam was the father, Tyler was supplying Liam with drugs and Liam had overdosed. The rumours became more and more wild. I tried not to take any notice. But what if there was a grain of truth? After all, I'd heard them arguing the evening before he died.

I pull up my knees and hug them close to my chest.

Whatever anyone says, it made no sense that someone as fit as Liam could have a heart attack; how a fatal medical condition could appear from nowhere. Did he know? Is that what he was hiding from me – was he too ashamed to admit he had a problem? Or was it something else? If only Liam had talked to me.

I stare at Kelly's message. Why now?

Then I look at Dad and sense a small shift inside me.

Why *not* now? Just because Dad hates the Dawsons, it doesn't mean I have to.

Gran thinks Kelly's party is a great idea. She's trailing round after me, making sure I give all the pots in her garden a good water. "It's time you started going out a bit more," she says.

"Even if it's Kelly?" I try to reach a hanging basket without pouring water all over my head.

Gran pauses. "It must have been terrible for that poor brother of hers. He and Liam were very close. To be honest, I think your dad was a bit heavy-handed. Do you still see Tyler at the running club?"

I shake my head. The last time I saw Tyler run, he was leaving the hospital on the day Liam died. He didn't seem to know which direction to head in. He caught my eye for a millisecond, took a couple of steps, then jumped a low fence and sprinted off. I'd never have caught up with him even if I'd tried.

"If Mum and Dad find out I'm going to a party at Kelly's, they'll kill me." For some reason I smile. Somewhere inside, the opportunity to do exactly the opposite of what they'd want is attractive.

"But they're not going to find out because they're not going to be here, are they?" Gran's voice is bland and neutral, as if she's discussing the weather. "I won't tell them if you don't." She winks and then surveys her small garden. I shake the last few drops of water out of the can. Mum once told me that Gran had a reputation as a troublemaker when she was young. It's not hard to believe sometimes.

"So you really do think I should go then?" I ask.

"It's your decision, Amber. As long as Simon is with you, I'm sure you'll be fine."

I've invited Simon. Who else was I going to ask? But I'm not sure he is going to be with me, though I haven't mentioned this to Gran. It's his sister's birthday this week and they're having a family party on Saturday night – Simon's not sure he'll be able to get away, or that's what he says. It all sounds a bit vague and I have a feeling he's just paying me back.

Gran appears deep in thought. At last she says, "I don't think Liam would want to see you sitting around moping. He'd prefer to see you out having fun."

"I can't remember how to have fun."

Gran puts her arm around my shoulders and gives me quick squeeze. "It's time you got back into practice, then."

I suppose she's right, but I'm not sure the anniversary of my brother's death is perfect timing.

CHAPTER 5

June 27th. The day I've been dreading.

It's 8.06 when I wake up. The numbers shine out from my phone.

Emptiness.

That's the first thing I sense – the emptiness of the house.

I lift my head then let it flop back down on my pillow and blink a few times, thoughts going this way and that, as I try to shape the day.

Mum and Dad left early to avoid the weekend traffic and, I'm guessing, the opportunity for Mum to get drunk. I should've gone to Gran's last night, but I thought I wanted to wake up here this morning. Now I'm not so sure.

I reach for Liam's stone and his voice rings clear in my head. I try to blank it out, but I can't.

"What the hell's got into you, Amber? I can't believe you stole my stone."

The words from that phone call will stay with me for ever.

"You look after it with your life and you give it back. If you let anything happen to it, I'll never forgive you."

I slip the leather lanyard over my head and slide the knot to tighten it, feeling the weight of the stone round my neck. I am looking after it with my life, I won't let anything happen to it. But now I can't give it back and Liam can never forgive me. I just wanted him to talk to me, that's all. I never meant for anything to happen.

I kick off the covers, stand up and open the curtains. The sun streams in and I let the warmth pour over my body, breathing it in. Was it sunny on the day Liam died? Why don't I know?

My head tells me to keep walking past Liam's bedroom door and go straight downstairs. My feet have a mind of their own. They drag me into Mum's room and towards the drawer where she hides the key to his room. I feel under her sweaters until my fingers close around the familiar metal shape.

Liam didn't always have a lock on his door. Not

until he complained to Dad that I kept barging in; that he had no privacy. That was rubbish. I never barged in.

I put my head against his door, telling myself not to go in, then slowly turn the key.

The room is grey, bare and still.

It's not Liam's room any more, not in any real sense.

The day after the funeral, Mum took all Liam's stuff to the bottom of the garden and burnt it. There must have been things she couldn't burn because I heard her tell Dad she'd taken them to the dump. I'll never forget the smell of smoke on Mum's clothes, the burn marks on the wooden fence, the pile of cinders and ash, Dad's face.

I stare out of Liam's window. Even now there's a rough circle of raw, blackened earth where the bonfire used to be. Nothing wants to grow there. Why did she have to destroy everything?

I'm seized by an overpowering urge to smash the silence.

I jump on to the bed and I bounce and whoop like we did when we were small and Dad used to go mad at us. Each time my feet hit the mattress, a spray of dust rises and twinkles in the air, and Liam's stone clunks against my skin. I laugh. For a moment I think I hear Liam laughing too and that stops me. It stops me, it folds me up and then it creates a pain so intense across my chest that I think I might be dying too. I flatten myself on to his bed and cry and cry until my sleeves are soggy and my head is thick with misery – until I can't cry any more.

"I was going to give it back," I whisper into his mattress. "But it wouldn't have made any difference. It was your heart that was the problem. That's what the doctors said." I want him to hear me. "It wasn't my fault. It wasn't anyone's fault. It was your heart." I say it over and over, hammering my fists on to the yellowing pillow. "It was your heart, it was your heart. . ."

When I find the strength to look up, the dust has settled and the sun is still shining. I know he hasn't heard me. Of course he hasn't. He's dead.

A loud bang followed by the sound of swearing comes from next door – that crazy dog of theirs knocking over the bin again. Next door, life is normal. In here it isn't and I need to get out. By keeping Liam's door closed, I can pretend he's on a long holiday, that someday soon he'll come back and I can say sorry and things will be all right again. By locking the door, I can lock away reality.

I decide to go over to Gran's sooner rather than later. Packing is an effort when you're not thinking straight and any enthusiasm I had for Kelly's party has gone. I stare into my cupboard. Kelly's always top-to-toe cool. God knows where she gets the money from. I open my bag and chuck in jeans, T-shirt, warm sweater, clean underwear and a toothbrush. I scrabble around for some make-up then recheck Kelly's text. Sleeping bag – don't have one. Drink – presumably alcoholic. For once, I'm thankful for Mum. I spend so much time trying to get rid of her bottles that I know all her hiding places. I hate the taste of alcohol. It reminds me of the smell of Mum's breath, the acid vomit, the dirty sheets. Still, it wouldn't be cool to arrive at Kelly's empty-handed. It takes me longer than I expect to find a bottle and I have to give Dad credit for his thoroughness. Luckily, he didn't think to check the "new" orange squash bottle. She thinks she's fooled me with that one, but she hasn't. I unscrew the top and take a sniff. Who says vodka doesn't smell? I shove it in my bag.

I wrap a scarf round my neck to cover the stone and check in the mirror to make sure no one can see it. I leave the house, lock the door and zip the keys carefully into the inside pocket of my overnight bag. I'm acutely aware of everything and everyone. Almost exactly this time, a year ago, Liam left this house and he never came back. I relive his last steps.

What was going through his mind?

At the bus stop I hold the secret of Liam's death inside me. No one else here knows what day it is today. I wonder what sadness each of these people are carrying around with them, because they all look pretty miserable.

Then again, the bus is very late.

CHAPTER 6

Kelly lives way over the other side of town and Gran's offered to drive me.

"You're looking very nice," she says as I come down the stairs. She'd say that whatever I looked like. I don't feel nice. I feel dull and uninspiring, in need of new clothes. Everything I own has memories attached to it: things Liam liked, things he hated, things I wore when we went certain places. The T-shirt I'm wearing now – Liam had one almost exactly the same. We laughed about it at the time. Sometimes I have a strange sensation of becoming my brother. Maybe I'm not yet ready to let him go, or maybe he's not prepared to let me go.

I wish more than anything that Simon and I could arrive at Kelly's together. I'm nervous on my own.

What if I don't know anyone? Will anyone talk to me? Will Simon turn up at all?

Getting to Kelly's takes an age. Gran managed to find me an old sleeping bag and the stink of mothballs fills the car. We follow the calm voice of the satnav. It's one of those ones you are supposed to stick to the windscreen – except Gran got it second-hand and it doesn't really stick any more. So I hold it in my lap and wait for the inevitable words, *You have reached your destination*.

"What number?" asks Gran, peering at the doors. It's a pretty rough street, rougher than where the Dawsons used to live round us. Gran's face gives away nothing, but I wonder if she's having second thoughts about letting me come.

"I won't park right outside," she says. "It would only embarrass you."

"Don't be silly," I laugh, "you're not an embarrassing kind of Gran." If Dad was here now, he'd be hammering on Kelly's door, demanding to see her mother. But Dad wouldn't be here because he wouldn't let me anywhere near the Dawsons' house. The thought makes me determined to have a good time.

"Make sure Simon looks after you," she says. "Do

you want to wait for him?"

I shake my head.

"And you know you can ring me at any time."

I nod.

"I mean it, Amber – any time at all."

Her worrying makes me more nervous. "I'll be fine," I say.

I lean over to give Gran a kiss then let myself out of the car. I grab my stuff from the back and kick the door shut with my foot.

"Have a lovely time," Gran calls out of the window. "And I'll pick you up at eleven tomorrow unless I hear from you otherwise."

"OK."

Gran gives a little wave and drives off. Too late to change my mind now. I hitch the sleeping bag under my arm and head towards Kelly's door.

Number 43. There's a window open at the front and I can hear voices inside – not many by the sounds of things. I ring but no one answers so I knock loudly. The door is opened by a tall, pretty girl I don't recognize. I hope I haven't got the wrong place. She looks me up and down.

"Is this Kelly's house?" I say.

"Depends who's asking."

51

"Amber," squeals Kelly from over the girl's shoulder. She comes and takes my hand, dragging me towards the kitchen. I nearly drop my bags in the process and she tells me to chuck them on a pile in the corner. I keep my small bag on me, looped across my body.

Kelly's looking great and I kick myself for not making more of an effort – though I'd never get anywhere near the way she's done her hair and make-up. It must've taken hours. The others are all dressed up too and it makes me feel doubly awkward. Kelly drapes one arm around my shoulders and flies through the names of the girls standing in the kitchen. They hardly bother to look at me. They're all too busy sipping their drinks and appearing somewhere between cool and bored. I try to memorize the names. I think the one in the shorts is called Zoe. I'm glad Kelly seems so pleased to see me.

She tells me there are masses of people coming, though there aren't many here yet. There's a group lounging around in the sitting room and the rest of us are with Kelly in the kitchen. No one seems to know quite what to do or say. Zoe keeps flicking her hair. Two of the group are whispering and they glance in my direction. I look away, my cheeks hot.

"Nice shoes," someone says to someone.

"Nice shorts."

"Nice nail varnish."

Conversations begin and fizzle out. More drinks are poured. There are various bottles on the bench-top and I slip off to get mine to add to the collection.

"What's this?" says a girl, pouncing on my bottle and wrinkling her nose. "Looks like orange squash." She laughs, shakes her head slightly and hands it to Kelly.

"*Is* it squash?" asks Kelly disbelievingly as she unscrews the lid. "I meant bring *alcohol*."

"Lame," mumbles one of the others.

Kelly holds it under her nose and sniffs. "Whoa! OK." She takes a swig, makes a face. "What is it? Vodka? Shit – you might've warned me it was neat."

The others giggle as Kelly splutters. "Can't be neat, Kell," says Zoe, "vodka's not that colour."

"Shut up. You try it if you think it's so funny." She holds it out to Zoe, who takes a huge swig before passing it on. They hand the bottle to me. I pause for a heartbeat then take a long swig and immediately regret it. It starts me coughing and makes my eyes water.

"Easy does it," says Zoe, taking the bottle back. She has another gulp without any obvious side effects.

The vodka earns me a few points – a sort of gap opens in the cosy circle and I'm allowed into it. Conversation starts to flow more easily: chat about people I don't know, places I haven't been, things that have happened at their school. I try to laugh in the right places, try to look interested.

A big group of boys arrives with boxes of beer. I see Zoe plucking at the back of her shorts with her fingers and I'm not sure if she's trying to make them longer or draw attention to her bum. The vodka has started to kick in and it makes me giggle.

"How did you get that here without your parents noticing?" Kelly asks them as they dump the beer on the side and help themselves.

"Who said anything about parents? That's what older brothers are for."

I tense up, immediately. I don't mean to but I can't help it.

"It's all right if you've got an older brother," says Zoe. "Mine's only seven, and he's a right pain. I caught him in my room the other day looking at my Facebook. I nearly killed him, I can tell you. I'm getting a lock on my door if he carries on like that."

I don't know if it's the day, the vodka or the mention of locked doors – or maybe a combination of all three – but I want to scream at her; tell her she's lucky to have a brother at all. I want to ask her how she'd feel if she got home tonight to find he was dead. I fight to keep my mouth shut and Kelly must see something in my face because she's beside me and pushing me across the room.

"Let's go and put some music on," she says.

"It's OK," I say.

"Clearly it's not." Kelly sounds quite aggressive.

"Sorry."

"No, *I'm* sorry," she says with a sigh. "I know what day it is and I'm sure you're sad. But now you're here, you may as well enjoy yourself."

That takes me by surprise – that she's remembered the date of Liam's death.

"I didn't think you'd come if I'm honest, but I thought the least I could do was ask."

I nod and force a smile. So she invited me expecting me to turn her down and now she's stuck with me. Perhaps I should leave now.

"Thought it might take your mind off things," she continues, as she plays around with the music.

"Yeah — well thanks for inviting me. It's nice to see you." I try to sound genuine. "Is anyone else coming that I know?"

"Doubt it. That's why I said to bring a friend. My friends have all changed. It's cool where I'm at school now."

"Simon may come along later. It's his sister's birthday so he's not sure. Do you remember him?"

She frowns as she scrolls through her playlists. "Kind of." With the iPod back on the docking station, Kelly turns up the volume and music thuds through the room. Someone waves at her from near the door and Kelly's face brightens. She waves back, tells me to have fun, and makes her escape, leaving me like a spare part.

I stare around. There's no one I know. Groups stand drinking, smoking, laughing. The brief warmth of the vodka has vanished, replaced by the cold knowledge that I shouldn't be here. Why did Kelly bother to ask me? I try joining in with a few groups but they blank me. One guy starts talking to me and offers to get me a drink but doesn't come back. I text Simon.

How long until you get here?

He replies. **No idea. That bad?**

I'm determined not to sound like a loser. **It's OK.**

It's hard to look comfortable when you're standing on your own at a party. I wander back to the kitchen in the hope that it might be better in there. It isn't, so I follow Mum's example and pour a slug of orange vodka into a plastic cup and find some lemonade to mix it with. I sip it steadily, the rawness biting at my throat. I pour another one and knock it back in one go. It's packed in here now, and the temperature and noise seem to rise with every passing moment. Some guy comes up and helps himself to a mugful of Mum's mixture and raises his cup. Automatically, I knock my plastic cup against his and the drink spills. I laugh and pour some more. Soon after a girl cosies up to him and kisses him and tries to drag him away. He shrugs and rolls his eyes at me, then follows like a lamb. The room is getting hotter. Halfway through my fourth – or is it my fifth? – I start to feel queasy. I put down my cup and push my way through the crowd, mumbling apologies as I hit people's elbows and spill their drinks. A trail of swear words follows me. I almost cry with relief when I find the toilet and see that it's empty.

I shut the door against the noise and lean my head

against the cool of the wall. Air. Give me air. There's a tiny window high above the toilet. I clamber, unsteadily, on to the seat and fiddle with the catch. It opens a little but there's some kind of security lock to prevent it being opened too far. I put my nose as close to the gap as possible and gulp in breaths. Slowly, the feeling of nausea and panic begins to subside, then I sit down and hang my head between my knees. My bag is heavy round my shoulders and I slip it off and put it on the floor. This is horrible. I try to work out what I'm going to do next. My only hope is Simon.

There's a loud banging on the door. "Get on with it can't you? What're you doing in there?"

The panic rises again and I get up quickly and flush even though I haven't even opened the toilet seat. The hammering goes on and there's more than one voice now. My face feels flushed as I ease open the door just a crack. Two girls eyeball me.

"About bloody time," one of them says and wrenches the door open, pushing past me to get in before shoving me out. A few people look in my direction and I feel worse than ever.

Stuff it. I'm getting out of here. I head towards the front door and feel around for my phone to ring Gran. My hand touches my shirt and my hip.

Where's my bag? For a horrible moment I think it's been stolen, then realize I've left it in the toilet. Why did I take it off in the first place?

I push my way back across the room, fighting my way through elbows and backs – not caring what anyone thinks this time. I try the handle of the toilet but it's locked, so I press my ear against the door. I can hear movement and giggling. I suppose I should be glad the same girls are still in there.

I wait. After a while I knock gently. Then louder.

"Go away!"

"I just need my bag."

"What bag would that be?" More giggling.

"Please, just hand it out. It's beside the toilet."

"Not any more it isn't."

There's a breathless silence and I stare hopelessly at the door.

"Come on," I say.

"Didn't your mummy ever tell you to take care of your things?"

Tears prick at my eyes and I give the door a sharp kick. A stream of swear words comes from inside. Angry, I swear back at them – empty threats.

I lean hard against the door, trying to force it open, but it's never going to work.

"I'm going to get Kelly," I shout at the door.

"Who's she?"

I fumble my way back into the living room, my sight blurred by tears. Kelly's nowhere to be seen. I ask a few people, but the most I get is a shrug. I force myself to think straight, to work out some kind of plan, but my head is about to explode and me with it. I don't know what to do. No one here is going to help me. If Kelly reckons her new friends are cool, she's wrong. I hate them all.

Someone touches me on the shoulder, fingers gently squeezing. Simon! About bloody time. Relief floods through me as I turn round.

It's not Simon.

"Hi, Amber. Kelly said you were going to be here." His eyes are a more piercing blue than I remember; his stare so intense that, for a moment, I can't find any words.

"Tyler?"

"Glad you remember me."

Remember him? Seeing him again detonates a minefield of memories. Tyler and Liam running, Tyler and Liam round at our place, Tyler at the hospital after Liam died. Kelly appears at his shoulder. "I thought we'd agreed you'd stay out of this," she says angrily into his ear.

"Don't worry, I'm not sticking around," he says. "Just catching up with Amber."

Kelly looks at me and frowns. "You OK, Amber?"

"Yeah, fine," I say brightly.

"Five minutes," she says to Tyler, "then I don't want to see you anywhere near this house."

Kelly gets swallowed back into the party and I look questioningly at Tyler.

"I'm not supposed to be here," he says, "but Kelly's parties are always trouble so I thought I should come and do a quick check. To be honest, I'd say this'd be a good time for you and me to get out of here."

"But why?"

"One of the neighbours will call the cops before long." He speaks quietly but urgently. "You're better off sticking with me." He looks around nervously.

"I can't leave. Two girls have got my bag in the toilet. It's got my phone in it – and money."

Tyler swears under his breath. "Wait for me by the front door," he says.

I'm so grateful to know someone and I can't wait to leave. I'm even more grateful when he reappears with my bag in his hand.

"How did you do that?"

He shrugs. "Did you bring anything else?"

"Yeah." What did I bring? "My overnight bag – somewhere at the bottom of that pile – it's the green one."

"Best not to leave anything lying around in here, for future reference," he says.

He throws bags aside as he unearths my green bag and the old sleeping bag.

"Come on," he says. "Time to go."

I'm swept along in Tyler's mission to get out of the place. I don't want to be stuck here if there's going to be trouble. He pushes me out of the door, and we hurry away from the house towards a battered grey car. Tyler throws my bag and kit in the back seat and I get in.

For a minute, I close my eyes and sink against the passenger seat.

"Looks like I arrived in the nick of time," he says, starting the car. "Are you feeling all right? You're not going to throw up or anything?"

I shake my head. My pulse is racing and everything feels a bit strange, but I'm OK. I register the weirdness of what's happening. I'm in a car with Tyler Dawson.

"Where are we going?" I say.

Tyler shrugs.

"Whose car?"

"Mine – while Dad's banged up."

I'm about to say, *again?* but manage to stop myself.

"I'm sorry," I say.

"What? Sorry Dad's in prison?" Tyler laughs through his nose, the air coming out in sharp puffs. "I don't know why they bother to let him out – a couple of months then he's caught stealing or dealing again and he's back inside. Anyone would think he likes the place."

I watch him as he drives. Something in my dulled senses tells me he cares more about his dad than he wants to let on.

"Does your mum know about the party?" I ask him.

"Sonia? She's Kelly's mum, not mine. I thought you knew that."

I shake my head. "Where's your mum then?"

"No idea." There's a nasty grinding as he shifts gear. "Sonia's all right. We get on better now I'm not living there any more. It was all a bit intense after . . . well, you know. Sonia must be nuts going away and leaving Kelly by herself after what happened last time."

"What did happen last time?"

"Exactly the same as what'll happen this time, and it's not pretty. I swear Kelly doesn't even know half the people in the house. Anyway, it's none of my business. As Kelly said, I wasn't supposed to be there."

"I don't think I was either. I don't know why she invited me; I don't know any of her new friends."

"Keep it that way. Anyway, it's good to see you."

I look at him shyly. It's been a while since anyone – apart from Gran or Simon – has told me that it's good to see me.

I clap my hand over my mouth. Simon! I'd better get hold of him. I'm pretty certain he isn't coming, but still, I should text. I twist around in my seat and reach for my bag.

"Shit!" I stare into my bag.

Tyler looks at me. I twist again, then undo my belt and get on my knees in the front seat and stretch down to the floor at the back, groping in the dark for my phone. It's awkward and now I do feel sick again.

"What's the matter?" asks Tyler.

I sit back round and try to swallow down the nausea. I can feel him watching me.

"Sodding phone's not in my bag. And I think I'm going to be sick."

Tyler stops the car and I get out, lean against a lamp post and take a few deep breaths. Tyler searches the back of the car again – under seats, in the pockets. Nothing.

"Those cows must've taken it," I groan. "Did they say anything? Didn't you check?"

Tyler makes a guilty expression. "Look, I'm sorry. I just got them to give me your bag. Didn't think you'd want me riffling through your personal stuff."

"My money too," I say, opening up my empty wallet. I flop back on to the seat, my arms limp at my sides. No money, no phone. Now what? Tyler does another quick search but I know there's no point.

"Here, you can use my phone," he says, handing me an old Nokia.

"Thanks," I say. But I don't know Simon's number. I don't even know Gran's. I start to scroll down through names. There must be someone I know – someone who might be able to help get Simon's number.

Tyler doesn't have a huge contact list. I recognize

a few of the names from school but no one who'd know Simon.

Ian . . . Kelly . . . Kyle . . . Laura . . . Liam. *Liam?*

A hundred thoughts run through my head – threads that I can't quite catch. Liam? I can't take my eyes off his name. I hold up the phone in view of Tyler. "Why have you still got this?"

"Different Liam," he says, reaching for the phone, cool as anything. I jerk the phone out of his reach and press *call*. Liam's voice. His message. Alive – here on the phone. Inside my ribs, someone has grabbed my heart and is squeezing it very, very hard.

"You shouldn't have done that," says Tyler. He leans over, calmly, and takes the phone.

I can't speak. All I can do is look at Tyler. I force myself to study him as a way of controlling everything else going on in my head. He's skinny to the point of being bony and his body is all angles in the driver's seat. His fair hair is shorter than I remember and badly cut. His features are the same, his cheekbones clearly defined and his jaw set rigid, as if he's clenching his teeth.

"Why did you just lie to me?" I whisper.

"It wasn't something you needed to hear. Especially not today."

"Today? So you remembered the date then?"

"It's hardly a date I'm going to forget."

I watch him bite his lower lip and I fold my arms across my front, trying to wrap up my own emotions.

"I wasn't going to go to the party," I say. For some reason I feel the need to defend myself. "I wish I hadn't now, but Gran said Liam would want me to go out and enjoy myself."

"Enjoy yourself on the day he died? Why would Liam want that? He'd be gutted."

My face flushes – part shame, part annoyance. How does he know what Liam would want? "*You* went to the party too," I point out. I don't see why there should be one rule for me and one for him.

"That was different," he says. I wait for him to explain but he doesn't. "What about your parents? I'm surprised they let you go."

"They didn't."

Tyler pauses. "They'd hardly be thrilled to find out you were at our place. Not after all the shit your dad threw around about our family."

I stare out the window. I should apologize to Tyler, but I don't know what to say.

"So what are you going to tell them?" he asks.

"Nothing. They're away."

Tyler turns and looks at me, looks back at the road, then back at me.

"Away?" he asks quietly. "This weekend? Without you?" He hits the steering wheel with both hands. "That's rough. They shouldn't have left you – it's not right."

The force of Tyler's reaction takes me by surprise and it scares me. Part of me is pleased that he's taking my side. The other resents his intrusion, the criticism of my parents, the criticism of me for going to the party.

"Mum's not well," I say. "Dad thought she'd be better if she was out of the house, that's all."

"And your gran thought you'd be better if you were out of the house. Let's all go out and avoid the issue – is that it?" His voice is weary, yet laced with sarcasm.

"I didn't know what to do, OK? All I know is that I didn't want to do nothing. Maybe I was wrong to come to the party. Maybe I should have . . . I don't know. Can't you understand? I – *didn't – know – what – to – do*."

He meets my eyes and then looks down. "I'm sorry," he says. "You're right. How could any of us know what to do?" He touches my shoulder with the tips of his fingers. "Anyway, let's look on the bright side; if you hadn't come to the party, I wouldn't have found you."

"You know where I live – you could've found me whenever you wanted."

"Like I was going to turn up at your place uninvited!"

I try to picture my dad's face if Tyler *had* turned up. Or if he could see me sitting next to Tyler now. My small act of rebellion gives me a buzz. A sense of power.

Tyler is watching me. His eyes take in every part of me and it's unnerving. I find myself unable to move, frozen by his gaze, faintly excited. Finally, he takes a deep breath and, without warning, grinds the car into reverse and manoeuvres backwards and forwards until we're facing the opposite direction.

"What are you doing?"

"What we should've done from the start."

"Which is?"

Tyler puts his foot on the accelerator and we jerk forward.

He drives fast now, too fast. I grip the edges of my seat, pressing my feet into the floor. Maybe this wasn't such a good idea. It strikes me how little I know about Tyler – my brother's best friend – the person who was with him when he died. I must be crazy sitting here beside him with no idea where I'm going. What if Dad was right? What if Tyler was somehow to blame? A traffic light goes red in front of us and he hits the brake hard. The signpost is clear. Tyler knows I've seen it. He glances at me nervously.

"Are you taking me where I think you're taking me?" I ask.

He shrugs. "Depends. I'm not much of a mind-reader."

I stare at the road ahead. I can almost see Liam's hearse in front of me. On the day of the funeral we crawled along behind it, all the way to the cemetery. I couldn't drag my eyes away from the blackness, the coffin with the flowers on top. And inside. . . I close my eyes against the memory.

"Please, I don't want to."

The light goes green and there's nothing I can do. I wait for the cemetery to come into sight: the cemetery where Liam is buried. I'd tried so hard to forget the rows of cold, grey headstones, the tidy grass, the moment I saw my brother's coffin lowered into the ground. My whole body begins to collapse in on itself.

Tyler slows a little. "It'll be all right," he says.

My heart is beating so hard, it's filling my throat. My ears are buzzing. I want to throw open the car door and run.

"I've never . . . this is the first time," I manage to stutter out.

"Please don't tell me this is the first time you've been back." I shake my head. "In a whole year?" His voice is a mixture of aggression and disbelief. "What about your mum and dad?"

"I don't know. They've never said anything."

"How could you abandon him like that? He's your brother! Well you're going to visit him now whether you like it or not."

"You don't understand."

Tyler angles the car into a parking space and gets out.

"Oh, I understand all right. You don't need to worry about that."

I can't move, can't even bear to look. This is what I've been hiding from. This is reality.

He runs round to my side, as if afraid I might try to escape. I would if I had anywhere to go. If I had money or a phone or some way of getting hold of

Simon or getting back to Gran's.

He opens the door and crouches down beside me. He puts one hand on my leg and smiles.

"It's OK," he says gently. "I promise."

I shake my head. How can it be OK?

"You said you didn't know what you should do," says Tyler. "This is what you should do — what *we* should do. Today. To show him we haven't forgotten him."

I cover my mouth with my hand and close my eyes to try to stop the tears. "Sometimes I wish I *could* forget him."

"Come on," he says, coaxing me out of the car. "You don't mean that."

The cemetery is heavily fenced with big metal gates. It closes at sunset and it's already way past that. I'm glad of the barrier between me and the graves.

"We can't go in," I say. "It's all locked up."

"I have a way."

Tyler knows where he's going and it's not towards the gates. "What if someone sees us?"

"They won't. No CCTV in this one." Tyler links his arm through mine. He doesn't slow up, even though I'm dragging against the pull. "I'm not going without you," he says. "Liam would want you here today. I know he would."

Would he? My hand goes to my throat where I check Liam's stone is tucked away under my scarf. The guilt is like a weight round my neck. It makes me bend forward as if walking into a strong wind.

We stop close by the fence and Tyler points to a small dip in the ground that's created a space underneath big enough to crawl through. "OK," he says. "Squeeze yourself through there." He checks around, presumably to make sure no one is watching. "Did you do this?" I ask.

He shakes his head. "Fox, I'm guessing."

I don't believe him. "What if we get caught?"

He puts his hand on my back and pushes me forward. "We're visiting your brother's grave. No one could blame us for that."

I give Tyler a doubtful look before lying down flat on my stomach and wriggling my way through. The earth is rough against my skin as my jeans pull away from my shirt. I watch as he slithers through in double-quick time, hops to his feet and flicks bits of dirt from his front. He sets off across the cemetery with me following. Tyler takes my hand and pulls me faster through row after row of old stones until we reach a newer part of the cemetery.

"How do you know where to go?" My whisper sounds too loud amongst the quiet of the graves. I'd have no idea how to find where Liam is buried. One grave looks much like another. So many dead people.

"Some of us visit regularly," he says.

"Us?"

He looks at me. "*I* don't like to think of Liam being alone."

The words hurt and I want to hurt Tyler back.

"He's dead," I say, my voice hard. I'm not about to tell him how I go into Liam's room, how I talk to him.

Tyler takes a deep breath – uneven and noisy. He stops and faces me. "You weren't there when it happened," he says. "I hate that I couldn't do anything. I hate that he's not here any more. Coming here helps me, that's all. I thought you'd get that."

I watch him struggle to control his emotions. I'd never stopped to consider the feelings of anyone outside our family, not really. I'd never thought of Tyler's grief. I reach out and touch Tyler's back and let my fingers rest there. He barely moves, barely breathes.

"I do get it," I say quietly.

Tyler sniffs. "Nearly there." We start to walk again. It's only twenty metres or so. In the almost-dark, he shines the light from his phone on the headstone in front of us.

I see Liam's name, the inscription that Mum and Dad discussed for hours and hours: *Run fast, run free,* and my breath catches in my throat. In front of the stone is a beautiful bunch of flowers standing in a large jam jar; attached to them, something written on a small card.

"Someone's already been here today," Tyler says.

"Not you?"

He shakes his head and we both crouch down.

"What does it say – on the flowers?" he asks.

I read it out loud. "To our most precious child. You are forever in our hearts. With love always. Mum and Dad."

When did they come? Early this morning? I imagine them standing here, together, placing the flowers on the grave. Suddenly everything I've been trying to hold in is expanding in my body, pressing at my bones and my skin and my head. The pressure pushes tears out of my eyes, slowly and silently. I don't even try to wipe them away. But I'm not crying for Liam, not like I was this morning. This time I'm crying for me. Because now I've seen it written down. Liam, their most precious child. Liam, the child who will always be in their hearts. I'll never be able to take his place. I don't deserve to take his place. I stand up and look at Tyler, see him wipe away his own tears with the back of his hand, and suddenly we are holding each other tight. We stand in the darkness, next to my brother's grave, holding each other and crying.

CHAPTER 7

There was something, as we stood there by the grave; something that drew us together and, for I don't know how many minutes, held us close. Now we're making our way back to the car, using the light from Tyler's phone, and whatever it was has gone. We're awkward, walking apart from each other. I don't know Tyler. He was Liam's friend, not mine. I didn't even like him very much. Now I don't know what to feel.

I shiver as I wait for Tyler to unlock the car. He starts the engine and puts the heater on.

"Let's go back to my place," he says.

"Gran's picking me up from Kelly's. I should go back there."

"I thought you were staying the night."

"Yeah – well . . . yeah." I can hardly argue, not

with my sleeping bag in the back. "But I ought to go back in case Simon's there. He'll be worried."

"There's no way we're going back there now, Amber. The place'll be wrecked. I suppose this Simon bloke is your boyfriend?"

I shift uncomfortably in my seat. "No."

"Then don't look so worried," he says. "I'm sure he can look after himself. It's only one night and I reckon we could both do with each other's company."

I tell myself to stop overreacting. I try to convince myself that Tyler is right.

"I've got two beds," he adds. His grin is kind of uncertain and apologetic. I relax a little.

"Where do you live?" I ask. "Is it far?"

"In a caravan on my auntie's farm. Well, not farm exactly, a couple of paddocks, more like. It's out of town a bit."

"Oh." I tell myself that this is all fine.

"It's pretty comfortable really – a bit basic. It's OK."

I massage the back of my neck with my hand, tipping my head forward then back. Tyler laughs a sad laugh.

"Liam used to do that – you know, massage the back of his neck when he was stressed."

I nod and smile a sad smile back.

"I'm sorry about everything that's happened," says Tyler. "I didn't mean to stress you out by taking you to the grave. I thought he'd like to know that we're together tonight, that's all." He takes a deep breath and then exhales loudly. "And I don't want to be on my own, to be honest. Too many memories."

He pulls my hand from my neck and I feel the cool dryness of his fingers. I let them twist and turn though mine, entwining our memories.

"I'll take you back to Kelly's tomorrow. No one need ever know you were with me. I doubt Kelly or any of her so-called friends will miss us."

I shake my head. I doubt they'll even notice we've left.

"I'll look after you," he says, looking straight at me for as long as he dares, given he's driving. There's something in his eyes – a sadness that makes me swallow. He needs someone with him. He needs me with him. Perhaps he's right, perhaps Liam would like it if we were together. Not "together, together" obviously, but in the same place.

"You have to promise you'll get me back to

Kelly's before eleven."

"Promise."

"OK." I'm too tired to think about it any more.

He lets go of my hand. I wonder what he would've done if I'd said no. We speed up and, before long, the street lamps and main roads give way to narrow lanes overhung with trees. We barely see another car. Eventually he turns on to a muddy track and we stop in front of a gate.

"Is this it? Are we here?"

"Yep. Would you mind opening it?" he asks.

I get out. Beyond the gate I can see only rough grass and a shadowy hedge-line. Pinned in the glare of the headlights, I fumble with the latch and try to work out how it operates.

"It won't budge," I shout over the noise of the engine.

"Lift it a bit."

I do as he tells me. The gate is heavy, but I manage to pull it up a little and the catch gives way with a bang, grazing my knuckles. I hold the gate open as Tyler drives through, then push it closed again with a loud clank that echoes in the quiet. We bump over rough ground until I see the greyish-white roof of a caravan behind the high hedge. We drive down a track parallel to the hedge until we come to a gap, then do something like a U-turn up the other side.

"Home sweet home," he says as he comes to a stop. He grabs his phone and swears. "Bloody thing's out of juice." He leaves the car engine running so he can use the headlights to see what he's doing. "I'll go and get us some light."

He walks quickly from the car to the door of the caravan, and seeing his loose, loping walk triggers a memory of him running. I can picture Liam by his side, their styles so different. Liam was a tidy runner, everything balanced, trained like a racehorse; Tyler more like a wild animal.

He struggles with the door, then disappears inside. In a few moments, I see a hazy, golden circle of light, followed by another. I watch him moving about, a shadow behind some thin material covering the windows. He doesn't reappear and I wonder if I'm supposed to go in. I open the car door just as he emerges.

"OK, we can see where we're going now," he says, switching off the lights and engine. The silence is huge. He picks up my overnight bag and carries it for me.

"Careful on the steps."

Inside, the caravan is lit by six small candles. Of course! Candles! Now I understand what took him so long.

"No electricity unfortunately," he says, noticing my gaze.

The whole place has a strange smell to it – not exactly nasty, more musty. I've smelt this smell before and I try to remember where. The floor is covered in patterned plastic and is dotted with brown circular marks, as if someone's been stubbing out cigarettes.

"You can have that bed," he says, indicating a seat along the right-hand side of the caravan. "I sleep here." He points at the seat on the left. They are separated by less than a metre. Between them is a folding table, the sides down. He lifts one side and the memory kicks in. Our holiday in Dorset twelve years ago. The last time I was in a caravan. My hand returns to my neck.

"Cigarette?" he says, removing a pouch from the drawer and beginning to roll the tobacco.

I shake my head.

"Still in training?" he asks, licking the edge of the paper and running his fingers along the length of the cigarette.

"No. Knee injury. You?"

Tyler laughs, but it's not a real laugh. "Not competitively. I try to keep fit, though." He holds a lighter to the end of the cigarette and inhales deeply.

The smoke in the confined space catches at my throat. I worry about the smell on my clothes and what Gran will say. She's made her views on smoking pretty clear. She caught me smoking in Granddad's shed when I was thirteen. Kelly said I needed some practice and that was where I went. Next thing I know Granddad's got lung cancer and he's dead. In my mind, his death is linked with my smoking. I haven't touched one since.

"Can I open a window?" I ask.

"Go ahead," he says, smiling.

The window has greyish moss growing on the inside. I unfasten the catch and push so that it opens just a crack. We sit in silence and when my stomach rumbles loudly, I wrap my arms around it, trying to hide the sound.

"Hungry?" Tyler says, laughing.

I blush. "No, no, I'm fine."

"Liar!"

He stubs out his cigarette and gets up. There's

83

a kind of compulsive speed to everything he does. "Food," he says. "I didn't think about food."

He opens and closes cupboards, pulling out cereal, milk, bowls, and spoons. I remember the big bag of crisps I've got in my overnight bag.

We sit opposite each other, munching on cornflakes. The milk is warm and tastes slightly sour. Then we eat the crisps. It's just after midnight. The anniversary of Liam's death is over. Here begins the second year. Here in a caravan with Tyler.

"What are you doing with yourself nowadays?" I ask.

"This and that. Minding the house for my aunt and uncle while they're away visiting their son in Australia." He doesn't quite meet my eyes.

"Australia? That's exciting."

Tyler shrugs.

"How long is your dad. . . ?"

"Five years. But I doubt he'll do that long. That's how it works – or doesn't work in the case of my dad." Tyler stares between his knees then reaches for his tobacco pouch again. "Anyway, tell me about you."

"Still at school."

He leans forward and stares into my eyes. "I

don't mean that. I mean what's this last year really been like. How've you managed?"

"Fine." I nod my head in a determined way and he sits back and smiles.

"Fine as in not fine?"

"Sometimes."

"So your dad is. . . ?" Tyler leaves a space for me to fill.

"Working. Away a lot. Determined to turn me into a runner like Liam, disappointed in me for never winning, angry at me for being injured. He wants me in the athletics squad."

"Nothing's changed then."

I raise my eyebrows. I'm not sure what he means.

"Your dad. He used to drive Liam mad with his competitiveness."

This is news to me.

"And your mum?" he says. "You said she wasn't well."

I crank my head back and stare at the ceiling. "Terrible." Saying it out loud makes me feel better. "She drinks all the time. Some days she doesn't leave her room. Dad pretends nothing is wrong and leaves me to deal with it." I can't believe I'm telling Tyler all this.

Tyler's got his chin on his hands, his elbows resting on the table. His face seems charged with an energy that's both unnerving and mesmerizing at the same time.

"So he's in denial," says Tyler.

"I don't know. Maybe."

"They're both in denial. You are too."

"Since when were you the expert?"

"I had some counselling after Liam died. They talked about stuff like denial."

"I wasn't offered any counselling." That's not quite true, I did have a meeting with a woman at school who told me I could come and talk to her at any time. I never did. I was too scared of what she might ask me.

"You didn't miss anything," says Tyler. "I stopped going. I needed to work stuff out for myself. It's one of the reasons I'm here."

I'd give anything to have Tyler's freedom — my own place to hide away from the world with no one to tell me what to do, no one's expectations to live up to, no responsibilities. Just being out here, in this caravan in the middle of nowhere, makes me feel different.

"You're lucky," I say.

He looks at me as if I'm mad, his eyes fixed on mine. I can hear his foot tapping up and down against the caravan floor. Suddenly he sits back. "You don't mean that," he says. "I don't think you could describe either of us as lucky."

Tyler's rapid mood change puts me on edge. I stand up and carry our bowls towards a small, round sink. Tyler follows.

"Leave them," he says. His hands are on my shoulders. I slide away from him and place the bowls carefully in the sink.

He backs off. "I'll get your bed ready. You can use the bathroom." He throws open a door to a room no bigger than a small cupboard. Inside is a grubby-looking chemical toilet. He grabs a candle and puts it on a little shelf. "You can brush your teeth out here in the sink." He turns and puts his foot on a small pedal on the floor and presses it up and down a few times. A thin stream of water comes from the tap, spraying the cereal bowls. "It's safe to drink," he says.

I get my toothbrush from my bag. It's uncomfortable brushing your teeth and spitting in front of a near-stranger and I keep my head low over the sink, scooping little handfuls of water into my mouth. Tyler pulls out the old sleeping bag and shakes it out on to the seat that will become my bed. I sense he is watching my every move. There's no obvious towel so I wipe my mouth on the back of my hand and go into the toilet, closing the flimsy door behind me.

Shut in this tiny room, I try to gather my thoughts together. A caravan, a candle for light, a boy I hardly know outside. How have I ended up here? I should be worried out of my mind, yet I'm strangely calm. Tyler and me, I feel we understand each other.

As I unzip my jeans, I hear the first cords from a guitar. I'm grateful for the noise and he's good. He keeps playing until I step back outside and then he smiles shyly and puts the guitar to one side.

"Don't stop. I like it."

He shrugs and pulls the guitar back towards his lap. I wrap my sleeping bag around me and curl up next to him. This time he sings: quietly, gently. I join in – in my head. Definitely not out loud.

Soon I'm drifting in and out of sleep.

"Here, lie down. You can use this," he says, handing me a pillow.

I don't undress – just unwind the scarf from my neck, crawl into the sleeping bag and put my head down.

Tyler's move is so sudden, so unexpected. He

throws off his guitar and leans over me, his hands near my throat. I'm frozen with fear.

"You've got it!" he says.

It takes me a few seconds to work out what he's talking about. I feel the leather cord dig into the back of my neck as Tyler clasps Liam's stone.

I sit up and Tyler's arm moves with me. He doesn't release his hold on the stone. His eyes are closed and our faces are inches apart. He is so still I wonder if he is OK. Then his lips are on mine. Kissing me.

I keep my eyes wide open, shocked by the suddenness of his move, too surprised to respond in any way. As fast as it started, it's all over. He looks at me as if he barely recognizes me and holds up both hands in front of him. He gets to his feet and stumbles out of the caravan, mumbling an apology. I place my hand over the stone and listen to the blood pounding in my ears. I lie awake in the flickering candlelight, the feel of his mouth on mine, conscious of every sound. My sense of calm has gone now. I think about going after him – telling him it's OK. Instead I lie awake. Minutes, maybe hours go by.

Finally the door opens and I close my eyes. He hesitates by my bed and I hardly breathe. I think maybe I'd like him to kiss me again, but he moves away and I hear rustling as he settles into his own bed; a quick puff of breath as he blows out the candle. It's very dark. I keep listening until his breaths lengthen and become even. Still I can't relax. I look at my watch. Two o'clock. The wind has got up and it creates a strange moaning sound as it finds ways through nooks and crannies in the caravan. It's an uneasy sound that holds me at the edge of sleep for too long.

CHAPTER 8

I need to get to Liam. He's standing in the distance, holding up his stone to the sky. I'm in great danger and I'm trying to run. But my legs won't move and Dad is there, and Tyler. I wake up with a pounding head and a racing pulse, my hand gripping the stone. At first, I'm not sure of where I am; if I'm truly awake or still half dreaming. I turn over and see Tyler sprawled over his narrow bed, his bare leg hanging off the side. Did last night happen? In the daylight, things always seem different, and it is daylight now, the sun streaming in the window.

I wrap my scarf round my neck then check my watch, check it again and leap off my bed.

"Tyler, wake up! Wake up!" I fight my way out of the sleeping bag and shake him. He grunts.

"For Christ's sake, wake up. It's twelve o'clock. Gran was picking me up at eleven. Get up!"

I search around for my shoes and other stuff.

"Whassamatter?" Tyler slurs out the words in a sleep-filled way.

"Come ON. You've got to get me back to Kelly's. How long will it take?"

He sits up, looks around and scratches his fingers through his hair.

"Amber?" He says it almost as if he's surprised to see me there. Maybe he is.

"It's TWELVE O'CLOCK."

"What?" He closes his eyes and shakes his head as if he's trying to work out what's going on.

"We need to go. NOW. We were supposed to be back at Kelly's by eleven."

Something registers in his eyes and he gets out from under a blanket, still without any real sense of urgency. He's wearing his T-shirt and underpants and I look away and bundle my stuff into my bag as he pulls on his jeans. I know I'm blushing so I hurry out to the car and wait for Tyler.

"Come on, come on," I say under my breath, willing him to hurry up. He comes, half hopping, as he tries to ease up the back of his trainer. He seems to have twigged that this is urgent and he's trying to do everything at once – unlock his door, lean over and unlock mine, turn on the engine, fasten his seat belt. I chuck my bags into the back and the car starts moving before I'm properly in. We bump over the field and stop. I run to the gate, fumble to get it open.

I have no idea where we are in relation to Kelly's house.

"How long?" I ask, again.

"Twenty minutes – maybe. Depends on the traffic."

"Can I use your phone?"

"Not unless you've found a way of charging a phone with a candle," he says. "I'll sort it when we get to Kelly's."

I want to scream with frustration. This is a disaster. Tyler looks terrible and his driving is more erratic than ever. I need him to go faster, but I also need him to concentrate. He doesn't speak, doesn't even mention last night. I play and replay it in my head and get more and more confused. We race through a light as it goes red. Luckily there's not much traffic and we arrive at Kelly's in less than twenty minutes.

There's no sign of Gran anywhere. As we approach Kelly's house, the front door opens and someone, a boy, is pushed out. I vaguely recognize him from last night. He staggers up the path and along the pavement – still drunk.

"Idiot," says Tyler.

The door opens again and this time it's Kelly's mum with an armful of bottles, which she slams into an open dustbin. She looks up and sees Tyler.

"What the hell are you doing here?" she asks. "Did you know this was happening?" She waves her arms frantically at the front of her house then she sees me. She looks at Tyler then back at me, then back at Tyler. "Amber! I've had your gran here half the morning. Where've you been? Has she been with you, Tyler? You'd better not be. . ."

"Give it a rest, Sonia," he says.

"Come with me," she says pulling me by the arm. "You need to call your gran right away. She's worried sick. I told her you'd be fine but, honestly, you should've let her know."

I start explaining about my phone but she's not listening. She passes me the phone in the house and a piece of paper with two numbers scrawled on it. I recognize Gran's writing. *Ring!* she says.

I dial the home number and wait. There's no answer. I try Gran's mobile. It rings and rings.

"KELLY!" Sonia shrieks, "Get off your lazy backside and help me clear up this mess."

I hadn't even noticed Kelly, spread over the couch, looking like death. She flicks a V-sign at her mum and makes no effort to move.

There's still no answer.

"Well?" says Kelly's mum.

"She's not picking up," I say.

Sonia pauses for a minute and presses her fingers to her temples. "I'd better take you home."

"I'll take her," says Tyler.

"You will not. You can stay here and kick Kelly into action. I've had enough of cleaning up this disgusting mess."

Kelly puts a cushion over her face and holds it there. The whole place is trashed. I feel sorry for Sonia.

"Give me a few minutes to tidy myself up a bit," she says.

Tyler seems uncomfortable anywhere near me and he disappears into the kitchen. Do I follow him? I feel like I've done something wrong. Was it last night? Or is it just his own guilt for oversleeping and not getting me back here on time? I sit down and close my eyes. Why can't life be simple for once? I try talking to Kelly but she barely manages a grunt. I have a quick look around for my phone but I know it's a waste of time. Still, it gives me something to do.

Sonia reappears with a clean shirt on and her hair brushed.

"I want all this sorted by the time I get back," she says, aiming her words in Kelly's direction. She may as well be talking to a brick wall. She pats her pockets and searches around for her keys.

On the way home, Sonia doesn't say much. She asks me a bit about running and stuff. I'm grateful to her for taking me home and I answer politely, but as we get closer and closer to Gran's, I feel worse and worse. I've really messed up this time.

"I hope Tyler looked after you all right?" Sonia says. She's looking sideways at me.

"Yeah, he did."

"He's a good kid. Honestly, though, I suggest you stay away from Tyler and my Kelly."

I glance at Sonia. This is Kelly's mum, Tyler's stepmum. What kind of a mum warns you to stay away from her own kids? Though seeing her house this morning, perhaps I don't blame her.

It's hard to get Tyler out of my head. I didn't even say goodbye to him. I play over each incident. The party, the cemetery, the caravan, the way he grabbed Liam's stone. The way he kissed me. Would I care if I didn't see him again? I register a small twinge somewhere deep inside me. I squeeze my eyes shut against it, but it won't go away.

We pull up outside Gran's and I ask Sonia if she'd like a cup of tea or anything.

"Thanks, but I think I'll be on my way. I'm not exactly flavour-of-the-month with your Gran as it is and I'm not sure you will be either. I'll leave you to it." She smiles a weary smile and gives a hopeless shrug.

I turn towards Gran's door and take a deep breath.

I knock and wait. Knock again, louder. I want to get this over and done with. There's no answer, which is odd as the car is in the driveway. I open the letterbox and shout. Maybe she's locked me out on purpose. I scan up and down the street in case she's gone out to the shop or something, but there's no sign of her. I'm not sure what to do, so I walk back down the path towards the road. There's frantic rapping on a window somewhere behind me. I turn around, trying to locate the sound. More rapping and I see the face of Gran's neighbour, Mrs Smalley, in the upstairs of the next door house. She's scrabbling to get the window open.

"Wait, wait!" Her shouts are muffled. Finally the window flies open. "Just a minute, I'm coming down," she says, breathless.

I walk round to her door and wait until she gets there. "Come in," she says, making frantic little hand signals as if she's trying to waft me in through her front door.

"I'm looking for Gran," I say. "Have you seen her?"

"Yes. Come on in and I'll explain."

There's an awkwardness to her that makes me suspicious and I immediately think something must have happened with Mum. But then why is Gran's car here?

Mrs Smalley shepherds me into her living room.

"Now sit down, dear. And don't get too worried."

That sends me into a complete panic.

"What's happened?" I want to press Mrs Smalley's "on" button or shake her to get her to start speaking.

"I'm afraid your gran's had a nasty turn. Worse than normal. They've taken her in an ambulance."

I stare at Mrs Smalley as she rubs her hands up

and down her skirt. It takes me a while to even speak. "What kind of nasty turn? When? How long ago?"

"About an hour ago now. It's lucky I was here. She was on her way to her door and then over she went, just like that." She makes a dropping motion with her hand and arm.

I actually feel the blood draining from my face. Everything heading downwards and downwards and making me dizzy and faint.

"She'll be all right, she's in good hands now." Mrs Smalley's voice is a low hum in the background. "Now you sit there and I'll make us a cup of tea." She heads for her kitchen and the comfort of the kettle. I try to place the pieces in the right order. Gran coming to pick me up. Me not being there. Gran getting in a state. Waiting. Finding her pills. Coming home. Me missing. Too much. Too much for her heart. I'm scared now. Scared for Gran and scared for me. What about Mum and Dad. Do they know? I've been here before. This is all too familiar.

"Could I use your phone?" I ask, standing in the door Mrs Smalley's kitchen and raising my voice over noise of the kettle. "I need to call my parents."

"Of course, of course. It's just there. On the side. Can you see it?"

My hands are shaky as I dial Dad's number. He answers.

"Amber? Where the hell have you been? We've been trying to call you."

"Dad. Wait. Have you heard about Gran?"

"Yes, of course we have! Why else would be on our way to the hospital?"

"Is she all right?"

Mum's voice comes on the line. "She's in intensive care. That's all we know. What have you been doing? You weren't answering your phone. You were supposed to start your shift at the café at twelve. Even Simon didn't know where you were."

I can't think what to say.

"Amber?"

I hear Dad's voice in the background mumbling about having to talk about this later.

"We're at the hospital," says Mum. "You're to go straight home."

"I want to come to the hospital."

"No. It's better you wait."

Better for who? I need to see Gran. I need to explain. I have to know she's all right. I have to be there. This time I will not be too late.

"Mum. Wait."

"We'll call you as soon as we know anything."

"You'll have to ring me on the home phone. My phone . . . it isn't working."

"We *know*."

"Tell Gran I love her. . ."

Mum's voice crackles out some words and contact is lost. Mrs Smalley comes past me with a tray and I follow her into the sitting room. My hand is so unsteady, I can hardly lift the cup without spilling the hot tea. Why did I lie about my phone? There was no time for explanations. That's why.

"Any news?" she asks.

"She's in intensive care." My voice is very small.

"I'm sure they'll have her back on her feet in no time." Mrs Smalley pats me on the arm.

I want to tell her no one got back on their feet last time this happened. Liam died – like Gran is going to die. Because of me.

I try to drink my tea but all I want to do is to get home in case Mum and Dad call. I've got no money for the bus, so I'll have to walk. I put down my cup on Mrs Smalley's neat little tray and thank her. She shuffles to the door behind me, rabbiting on about her thoughts being with the family. I say goodbye and start to walk.

If only I hadn't left my bag in the toilet. If only Simon had been with me. If only Tyler hadn't come to the party. If only I hadn't gone with him, overslept, not been at Kelly's when Gran arrived. If only I could turn the clock back and do it all differently. Right from the start. From the day Liam died. How could I be so stupid? Gran can't die, she just can't. Down the hill and round the corner, one house blurring into another. I know this route backwards, could do it with my eyes closed. At the main road, I hardly look up. A horn shrieks and I feel someone pulling me back on to the kerb.

"Watch what you're doing," says a man, holding the back of my shirt.

Cars whizz past and I'm sucked towards them. One step. That's all it would take. I could get rid of all this in one step. So easy. But somewhere, deep inside, I know that it's not the answer. I take a deep breath, take one step away from the kerb and wait for the beep, beep, beep of the signal on the pedestrian crossing.

By the time I get home, I'm light-headed and dehydrated. The house looks grey and empty. Mum's window boxes, which used to be her pride and joy, are filled with the spiky-looking skeletons of last year's flowers. I bend down and open the zip of my overnight bag, then search around for my keys.

This is ridiculous. I push my fingers into every corner, pulling out the contents. I shake out my sleeping bag. Search again. They're not there. This is crazy. If they'd been in my handbag, I could understand. But they weren't.

"Looking for these?" says a voice behind me.

I turn round and Tyler is standing there, my keys dangling from his finger.

I puff out my cheeks as panic dissolves into relief.

"What. . . I mean, how come you've got my keys?"

"I found them on the floor of the car."

I flop forward and laugh. "THANK YOU," I say. "Really, thank you."

"They must've fallen out of your bag." He walks towards the door, putting the keys in my outstretched hand.

"How did you know where to find me?"

"As you rightly pointed out last night, it's not as if I don't know where you live."

"Yeah I know that, but how did you know that I was here – like now?"

"I've been waiting. I guessed you'd have to come

back at some point. I couldn't phone you. So I thought I'd better just turn up."

"You've been waiting?" I look at him questioningly. "You could have been waiting for a long time; I'm supposed to be with Gran." I close my eyes as I say her name.

"But she's not well."

"You know about Gran?"

"Only that she's in hospital."

I frown. "How would you know that?"

Tyler spreads his hands. "So this bloke Simon – your friend – was round at our place and he's had a call from your mum saying your gran is in hospital and does he know where you are – or something like that."

"Stop – STOP! Simon is round at Kelly's?"

"Not any more he's not."

"But he was?"

"Seems like it. He was asleep upstairs when I found him."

"So he was there, this morning, when we turned up?"

"Yeah, I guess. He wasn't in a great state."

"Shit." I can't believe Simon was there, at Kelly's house. So he did turn up last night. And he stayed

over even though I wasn't there? And got drunk –
apparently? This doesn't sound like the Simon I
know.

"What did Simon tell Mum?"

Tyler shrugs. "Nothing. Said he had no idea
where you were. Sounded pretty pissed off if I'm
honest."

I sigh. Can this get any worse?

"You didn't tell him, did you?" I say. "About
where I was?" If this gets back to Mum and Dad
there'll be real trouble.

Tyler laughs. "No, didn't say a word. Thought it
was best if I stayed out of it."

I nod an unspoken thank you at him. "And Kelly.
What did she say?"

"Not much. She's not good with a hangover.
Simon was trying to extract information from her
and it was going nowhere. I thought I'd better leave
and that's when I spotted your keys on the floor of
the car."

I fumble with the keys in the lock. Tyler is right
behind me and the closeness of him sends a tiny
ripple through my body.

"So is your gran going to be OK?" Tyler's voice
is full of concern.

"How would I know?" I snap. I fumble with the lock and realize I'm attempting to open the door with the café key. I'm angry with myself, not him.

"I'm sorry," I say, turning to face him. "She's had a heart attack. She's in intensive care. I'm waiting for an up date from Mum and Dad."

Tyler looks at the sky and I cover my face with my hands – my self-control collapsing. "If we hadn't overslept. . ." It comes out as a desperate wail.

He touches my shoulder but takes his hand away again quickly. "Don't say that!"

"It's true."

I turn and unlock the door using the right key. Tyler stands on the path, hands in pockets, head down.

"These things happen," he says.

"They happen to *me*. They don't happen to other people."

"Can I come in?" he says. "I mean only if you want me to. I understand if you don't."

I'm pleased he wants to stay, and I stand to one side to let him in. He stops in the hallway, looks around and clears his throat.

"It's different," he says.

"Different to what?"

"Different to when Liam was alive." As we walk into the kitchen he gives a small shiver, as if trying to shake off the memory. I don't know what he's thinking about because nothing has moved or changed.

"Drink?" I ask, pouring myself a glass of water.

"Thanks."

I pull a glass down from the cupboard and hold it under the tap.

"Is his room still . . . you know?"

I shake my head. "There's nothing much left. Mum burnt it all."

Tyler frowns. "Everything?"

"Not the furniture, that's still there, but everything else."

"Jeez." He runs his fingers through his hair and rubs the back of his head. "Do you ever go in there?"

"Sometimes. Mum keeps the door locked, but I know where she's hidden the key."

He walks about, touching things. Looking.

"Can I see it?" he says.

I pretend to search for biscuits in the back of the cupboard. I suddenly feel very possessive over Liam. I'm not sure I want to share his room with anyone else. I'm not sure I want to share Tyler with anyone else.

"There's nothing to see."

"Still."

"I can't."

He picks up an old tankard that Dad keeps on the side, stares at it and puts it down again. I close the cupboard and watch him. He takes a couple of steps in my direction and touches my hand, very lightly. "If you don't want to, that's fine." My skin tingles. I meet his eyes and I'm confused. Tyler looks uncertain too.

Maybe he senses me wavering.

"I just think it might help me," he says. "You know, to move on – or whatever it is they say."

I look at his hand on mine and I find myself nodding.

Tyler follows me as I climb the stairs. Outside Liam's, he stops. From the entrance of Mum's room, I watch as he leans forward and rests his forehead against the door.

"Wait there," I say. "I'll get the key." I'm not sure he hears me. I don't rush finding the key. It seems only fair to give Tyler a bit of space. This must be hard for him, coming back for the first time. It's odd that someone who was so often with Liam is almost a stranger to me – though not quite such a stranger as he was yesterday. Now I wish I'd had the chance to get to know him better. I remember Mum complaining that he and Liam spent too much time on the computer, that the music was too loud, that they never put their plates in the dishwasher. She could hardly moan at them for not taking enough exercise with all the running they did. *They're boys*, was Dad's answer to everything. When Tyler was around, the rest of us could go take a running jump – that was the message. And it still hurts, even thinking about it. But now there is no Liam. . .

I walk back with the key. Tyler is waiting. I unlock the door and let Tyler open it. He pushes it slowly, as if fighting an invisible force on the other side. I'm not sure whether or not to leave him alone.

"Shit!" he says, staring around as if trying to make some sense of what he's seeing. "This is terrible." His voice is almost a whisper and he folds his arms, hands gripping his biceps. He turns slowly, examining each part of the room.

"That signed poster he had of Mo Farah?" he says pointing at a place on the wall above Liam's bed. "That could've been worth something. And all his books and his football stuff."

"He didn't even like football," I say.

"I know. Still, he'd never admit that to your dad, would he?"

We share a smile.

Tyler lifts up the corner of the mattress and appears to search. "Everything's gone."

I wonder what he was expecting to find, but I don't ask.

He runs his hands along an empty shelf. "I wish your mum hadn't done this."

"Me too."

I sit down on the edge of the bed. Tyler touches the walls and trails his fingers over the bare furniture. Tiny movements as if testing the truth of what he's seeing. Finally he flops flat down on the bed, head on the brown-stained pillow, staring up at the ceiling. I pull up my knees and hug them to my chest. The air between us hums with tension, an almost magnetic force holding us close but not letting us touch.

"I know Liam wants us to look after each other." Tyler's words are directed at the ceiling.

"What makes you so sure you know what Liam wants?" I rest my chin on my knees. "He's not here any more. We both have to accept that." I say it as much to reassure myself as to try to convince Tyler.

His first touch makes me close my eyes. I dare not move. His thumb makes little circles at the base of my back then, slowly, he traces my spine all the way up to my neck and back down again. Every part of me focuses on the sensation – every nerve, every muscle, every thought.

"You and Liam are very alike." His arm slides around my waist.

I turn to look at him. "Are we?"

He lets go of me and shifts his hands to behind his head. Tingling anticipation is replaced by aching disappointment.

"Do you think he can see us?" he asks.

"Don't be silly," I laugh. I look around, half expecting to see Liam watching us from some shadowy corner. I'm not sure I want Liam's intrusion in this part of my life. I'd like to keep something for myself. God knows, he seems to control every other aspect.

"I reckon he'd be happy if he could." Tyler's voice is slightly husky. Like his singing voice.

The room is quiet but I know he is looking at me. More than looking at me – looking inside me. As if checking to see that what I'm feeling is the same as he's feeling. He cares about me. He cares that I'm here with him. I can sense it so strongly that it makes the pit of my stomach numb.

"Come here," he says.

I hesitate, nervous, but incapable of resisting. I stretch out beside him so we are both lying on our backs, staring up at the ceiling. Then he puts his arm across me and pulls gently, trying to roll me towards him. I don't give in right away. He laughs and uses more effort. I'm desperate to feel someone close to me – to feel Tyler close to me. I want to be wanted. I shift my body so I'm nestled against his side. We don't kiss or anything. We just lie on the bed together, my head on his chest. He has one arm around me, the other curled so his fingers rest on Liam's stone at my neck.

All I can hear is his heart beating.

CHAPTER 9

I don't know how long we lie there for. I feel calm and I don't ever want to move. The shrill tone of the phone breaks the spell and I leap off the bed, launching myself towards the door and down the stairs.

Four rings, five rings, six.

"Hello," I say breathlessly.

It's Dad's voice, slightly fuzzy. They're on their way home, apparently. Gran is in a serious but stable condition. I'd better have some answers ready — that's what he tells me.

Calm has vanished. Answers to what? How much do they know?

I have to get Tyler out of here.

I race back up and Tyler is already on the landing. "Shall I lock it?" he asks looking at Liam's door.

"I'll do it. You have to leave. My parents are on their way back."

He nods.

The softness in Tyler has gone, any sense of closeness replaced by an awkward distance. I find it hard to know what to do or say.

He follows me back down the stairs.

"When can I see you?" he asks.

"Do you want to?"

He flicks the palm of his hand with his fingers. "Of course I do," he says, taking a step towards me and touching my cheek.

"OK." I try to stifle a small, nervous giggle. "I'd like to see you too."

He smiles, opens the door and jogs the few steps towards his car. "See you soon then. Hope your Gran's all right." He doesn't say goodbye – just climbs in and drives away.

The air around me vibrates with his physical energy. There is a definable space where he was standing. I'm clutching the keys to Liam's room in my hand. Why am I shaking? I take the stairs two at a time. I mean to lock Liam's door, but once again I'm drawn in. I lie down on the bed, the mattress still warm, and try to feel Tyler's arms around me.

The last twenty-four hours race through my head. I'm tired, very tired, and I have to fight the urge to close my eyes and sleep. I force myself off the bed and out of Liam's room, replacing the key in Mum's drawer and covering my tracks carefully. My footsteps on the stairs are heavy as I hear first one car door bang and then a second. Mum and Dad are back.

Something, some unconscious gesture, takes my hand to my neck. Liam's stone! Visible so everyone can see it. I whip it off and stuff it in my bag as the front door opens.

Dad fills the door frame. Mum stands behind him, grey and fragile. I blush with guilt before anyone has said anything.

"How could you do it?" she says, her voice barely audible.

I retreat as they walk in.

"We talked to Simon," says Dad. "We know you were at Kelly's party. KELLY'S, for heaven's sake. What could've possessed you? Did you stop to think for one minute? Going off partying when you were supposed to be with your Gran. And on the day . . . on the day. . ."

"On the day Liam died?" I say. For some reason

being with Tyler has given me the strength to say the words. Dad glares at me.

"All those messages Gran left for you," says Mum. "Trying to find you – telling you to get in touch. I don't understand how you could ignore her – or us for that matter. You can't imagine how worried we were. No one knew where you were. Gran can't deal with that kind of stress."

"And nor can we," adds Dad. "But you're too selfish to think of that."

"You don't need to rub it in!" I shout. "For your information, my phone was stolen. I didn't get any of Gran's messages and I had no way of contacting her – or you."

"Your phone got stolen?" Dad asks with massive sarcasm. "Why am I not surprised? Trouble at the Dawsons'? Well, well! The point is—' and Dad points at me to underline what he's saying "—you should never have been there in the first place."

"Gran told me to go."

"Don't lie to us, Amber."

"I'm *not* lying. She thought it would be good for me to get out and enjoy myself for once."

"So where were you then? Why weren't you there when she came to pick you up? Hmm? Hmm?"

Dad's tone rises and rises. I can't think of an answer.

"Who were you with, you little—"

"Derek!" says Mum, taking his hand. He shakes it off, staring at me, wide-eyed. Then he turns on her.

"And you've changed your tune. One minute you're blaming Amber for everything, next minute you're taking her side. I've had enough of this family."

Mum pushes past us and heads upstairs.

"That's it, go and get drunk," shouts Dad behind her.

I know it's not even worth trying to talk to Dad when he's in this mood. I skirt past him and head up towards my room.

"This is all I need," says Dad and his tone of voice makes something snap inside me.

"All *you* need!" I say, turning round and stamping back down the last few stairs towards him. "That's all you think about, isn't it? What *you* need. Have you forgotten that Liam was my brother as well as your precious son? Ever since he died, I may as well have not been here – apart from your stupid running schedules. You've never stopped for one second to ask me how I feel; if I'm OK. And for your information I am *not* OK. Gran was trying to encourage me to have some fun again. She said it was what Liam would want."

"Go to your room, Amber."

"And, in case you haven't noticed, Mum is not OK either. She needs proper help and the sooner you recognize that the better. In fact, perhaps it's YOU that needs help."

Dad is still now. The air crackles.

"Go to your room now," he says quietly.

Shouting is fine, quiet is scary. I take three steps backwards. "You can stop telling me what to do, because from now on I'm going to do what I want," I say.

He walks towards me, threatening.

"NOW!" He blasts it right in my face, pointing with his arm outstretched up the stairs. I hesitate for another moment. Dad's never hit me before and part of me wants him to hit me now – to lash out and make some form of physical contact. He doesn't, so I turn slowly and walk up the stairs away from him. I feel cheated.

"And you're grounded for the rest of the summer," he shouts after me. "Do you hear me?"

Of course I hear him, how could I not with him yelling his head off? I don't bother to reply. How can he ground me for the rest of the summer? He's not here half the time. I slam my door and throw myself on to the bed. Anger pulses through my body in great waves. Someone had to tell him, didn't they? I thump the pillow with the unfairness of it all. And in among all this, neither of them has told me anything about Gran. I lie there, alternately seething and sad and sick. Sick of everything.

Anger turns to remorse and remorse to self-hate. I sit up late into the night, tears dripping off my cheeks as I make a card for Gran. I remember summers in the garden where Mum would unravel lengths of old wallpaper and Liam and I would stand in trays of paint then jump and run and stamp all over it. That was when life was simple; when we were a proper family.

"GET WELL SOON," I write across the top.

Perhaps she doesn't want to get well. Perhaps she's had enough of all this too.

I don't know what to write inside.

Please get better. I am so sorry I wasn't there when you came to pick me up. I will never forgive myself — not ever and I'll make it up to you, I promise. Please come home soon. I miss you. Amber XXXX

I do some underlining. I underline "so" and

"never" twice and "Please" three times. It makes me cry all over again. Then I look at it and I'm angry because it sounds like it's written by a three-year-old. But it's too late now so I put it in an envelope and seal it up. I don't want Mum or Dad to see what I've written.

I listen at my door to make sure neither of them are around, then creep to the bathroom. Brushing my teeth makes me think of the caravan and Tyler. I look at myself in the mirror: my pale face, my hazel eyes. The sun has brought out more freckles than usual.

I refuse to go down for supper. I lie on my bed, wrap my arms round my pillow and try to think of Gran. "Get better," I whisper over and over again. My mind keeps drifting from Gran to Tyler: the way he held me in the cemetery, lying together on Liam's bed. I'm fascinated by him. Knowing he is out there makes me feel less alone. He's the only person who's ever really talked to me, straight up, about Liam. I envy Tyler in his caravan. He's right, we do need to look after each other, because no one else is going to look after us.

CHAPTER 10

I don't know when I last ate properly. I pray Gran is still alive. I wonder what on earth I am going to say to Simon – how I'm going to explain. And I wonder how I can contact Tyler and if he was being serious about seeing me again.

I hope Dad might've left for work, but he's still in the kitchen when I come down. He raises his eyes from his cereal bowl and then lowers them straight away, as if the sight of me makes him feel ill.

So this is how it's going to be.

I pour myself a bowl of cereal. "Any news on Gran this morning?" I ask, terrified of the answer.

"She's the same. A little better. They're moving her to the high-dependency unit later today."

I exhale – I must've been holding my breath. "Does that mean I can visit her?"

"She doesn't want to see you, Amber."

I stare at him.

"Can you blame her?" he continues, keeping his eyes on his newspaper, pretending to read and talk at the same time. "No, the best thing you can do for your grandmother is stay away. We've told her you're all right. "

I keep staring at him for a long few seconds. I hate him. I'm not stupid. I get why Gran doesn't want to see me. I just want the chance to explain so she can understand what happened. I just want the chance to say sorry. I go to the fridge to get milk. There's none and I look around, finally spotting the empty bottle on the table next to Dad's bowl. I sigh.

I spoon dry cereal into my mouth, hoping he'll notice.

When Mum comes down, she's showered and dressed and her hair is clean. Dad smiles and tells her she's looking nice. She's looking sober, so that's something.

"We're leaving in twenty minutes," Dad snaps at me. "You'd better go and get ready." I stop midway through a mouthful.

"So I *can* go and see Gran, then."

"No," he says, slamming his paper down on the

table. "I'm going to drop you at work first and then take Mum on to the hospital. I need to make sure you are where you are supposed to be."

Mum puts out her hand to Dad and he takes it. "Do you have to work today?" she says to him. "I could do with the support."

"Sorry, love. I'd like to stay, you know I would, but these meetings are important."

I could come to the hospital, I think. I could support you – if only you'd let me. But I dare not say it out loud.

"Will you be all right getting home?" he asks Mum.

She nods. "I'm going to stay at her place. It's closer to the hospital There are things she'll need me to collect and she'll be worried about her plants and the cat being left alone."

"Aren't you back tonight then?" I say to Dad.

"No. I'm working. And don't you go getting any ideas. You're grounded – remember?"

"Where are you going this time? Surely you can get time off if you tell work what's going on?"

Dad narrows his eyes and explains in a clipped voice. "I'm up to Manchester tonight then on to Birmingham tomorrow. I'll be back on Wednesday.

Someone has to keep the food on the table."

So Dad's away and Mum's more worried about leaving the cat alone than me.

"As long as the cat is OK," I say. "I'll feed myself. Perhaps you could bring back some milk." I tip the rest of my cereal in the bin.

Mum sighs and Dad stands up and gives her a hug. "I suppose we can trust you to behave, Amber?" asks Mum. They both look at me.

"I suppose."

"You are not to go out," adds Dad. "Do you understand? When I say grounded, I mean grounded."

"Does that count going to work? I thought you said you were dropping me off."

"Don't start," says Dad. "We don't need any of your attitude. Work is work and Cathy'll let us know straight away if you don't turn up."

"And no one is to come round here either," says Mum.

"Like I'd ever invite anyone to this dump," I mumble. I can't remember when I last invited friends round. I haven't dared – I never know what state Mum is going to be in. That's probably why I don't have any friends any more.

"Ten minutes," says Dad. "I suggest you go and get ready."

We struggle through the morning traffic and Dad keeps checking his watch. He doesn't bother to park when we get near the café, just tells me to get out at the lights.

"Will you give this to Gran for me?" I hand my card to Mum.

She takes it as the light goes green and I only just manage to slam the door before Dad drives off.

"Bye," I say to the rear of the car as it disappears across the lights and down the street. I spin round on one foot and make my way to work. Now I've got to face seeing Simon and explain myself to him. I'm not too worried. He'll understand. In fact, I'm quite looking forward to hearing his version of events.

The smell of coffee and baking fills the café and my stomach somersaults with hunger. "I'm certainly glad to see you," says Cathy. There's a hint of annoyance in her voice.

"Sorry about yesterday. My phone got stolen and then Gran. . ."

Cathy softens. "I know. Your mum says she's doing a bit better. Knowing your gran, she'll be back on her feet in no time."

"Fingers crossed."

Cathy holds her hands in the air so I can see her crossed fingers. I make myself a large mug of coffee and pinch a couple of croissants stuffed with cheese and bacon.

"So what's going on with Simon?" she asks.

I stop with the croissant halfway to my mouth. I look at my watch.

"He's late," I say. I take a huge mouthful and swallow before adding, "Probably still recovering from his hangover."

"So he hasn't told you then?"

"What – about the weekend?"

Cathy carefully folds a dishcloth. "He's handed in his notice. Well – not notice, exactly. He's left."

I almost choke. "He can't do that!"

"Unfortunately he can. He says he needs a break." She's still looking at me.

"You're joking, aren't you?"

Cathy shakes her head. "I thought you might know what was going on." The way she says it makes me think she knows more than she's owning up to.

"He turned up late yesterday, with – as you say – a terrible hangover and in a filthy temper. At the end of the afternoon, he told me he wouldn't be coming back. I asked him why and he told me to ask you. He left half his stuff here so I thought he wasn't serious. But he's rung in this morning to say he'll be picking up his things before the café opens." She looks at her watch.

"And he said to ask me? Why?"

"That's what I hoped you'd tell me." She keeps folding her clean dishcloths into neat squares.

"I'll talk to him," I say. "He'll change his mind."

"Let's hope so. We don't need to be losing experienced staff over the summer."

My hunger has vanished. I can understand that Simon would be pissed off with me, but I can't understand why he'd leave the café. It's good pay and he enjoys it – or that's what he's always said. I wonder if it's something to do with Mum. I don't have much time to think about it because the door opens, Simon walks in and he stops dead. He's obviously surprised to see me – and not in a good way. He stands in the doorway, neither in nor out.

"What're you doing here?" he asks. "I thought you'd be at the hospital."

"I'm not allowed to visit yet."

Cathy appears from the kitchen. "Right, you two. I'm giving you twenty minutes. Go away and sort this out. Go on – off you go."

She kicks us out the door like a couple of naughty dogs. Simon starts to walk and I follow along behind. Maybe I'm angry with myself, I don't know, but Simon's behaviour makes me feel both defensive and aggressive at the same time. Can't he see he's just making a bad situation worse?

"I'm sorry about the party," I say, gruffly. "I didn't know if you were coming or not."

"I said I'd come, didn't I? I'm not the kind of person who lets people down at the last minute."

He doesn't bother to add "*unlike some*" and I roll my eyes. First point to Simon.

"My phone got stolen, I couldn't call you."

"So I hear." He manages to sound one hundred per cent unconvinced.

I spread my hands. I'm telling the truth. It's not my fault if he chooses not to believe me.

"So where were you?" he asks. "I was worried."

"Not worried enough to stop *you* having a good party, from what I've heard." I know I'm dealing with this all wrong, but I can't stop myself.

He pulls me to a halt. "I waited. I thought you'd come back. You weren't answering your mobile, I tried you at home. OK, so maybe your phone had been nicked, but where were you?"

"I stayed the night with a friend."

"A friend? What friend? I thought you didn't know anyone. You were supposed to be staying with Kelly."

I look at the ground.

"So who was it?"

"Someone I used to know."

"Oh, come on, Amber. Who were you with?"

"Tyler."

"Tyler Dawson?"

"What's wrong with that? He turned up a couple of hours into the party. He said the police would come and shut it down and we needed to leave if we wanted to stay out of trouble. I couldn't call you or Gran, so I went back to his place. What else could I do?"

"I didn't see any police."

I shrug. "By the way, thanks for telling Mum and Dad I was at Kelly's."

Simon shakes his head and sits down with his back against a wall. I stay standing. "I had to," he says.

"What else could I do? Your gran was in hospital. No one knew where to find you."

He tips his head back and closes his eyes. We get a couple of funny glances from passers-by. We must look odd, the two of us there together, not speaking.

"I'm sorry," I say. "I messed up, I know that. You're not really going to leave the café, are you?"

He opens his eyes again. "I already have."

"Just because of Saturday night?"

"No – not just because of Saturday."

I wait, arms crossed.

"So here's the thing." Simon clears his throat. "I like you a lot. More than a lot. I know we've been friends for ages, but I thought . . . I mean, I know it's hard to move from that into any kind of relationship. . . It's just, I can't. . . Anyway, I think it's time for me to move on." He lapses into silence.

My imagination fills in the gaps. I guess I've known for a while and now I feel guilty. I want him as a friend, he wants something more. Maybe I've even encouraged him, but the simple fact is that I like him, but I don't fancy him.

"I thought maybe you needed time after Liam died," he says, "I didn't want to push anything. And then when you went off with someone – with

130

Tyler – at the party, I guess that proved that I'd been waiting for nothing. I can't watch you being with someone else. I can't help how I feel about you. I wish it could be different, but there we go."

"Nothing happened between Tyler and me – you've got that wrong." I feel myself blushing even as I say it.

He looks at me, smiles and shakes his head. "I'm not stupid."

"So you're chucking in your job at the café because of a bad guess about what happened on Saturday night? That sounds stupid to me."

"I'm chucking in my job because I don't want to see you for a while. It's too hard. I'll get over it, but I need to give myself a break."

"But we can't not see each other."

He looks up at me and the hopelessness on his face says it all.

"And we need you at the café."

He shakes his head, sadly as if I just don't get it. But I do get it. I hate that I've made him so unhappy. But what am I supposed to do? It's not my fault he wants something different to me. I can't pretend I fancy him. Why can't we carry on like before? He's my best friend – *was* my best friend.

He heaves himself back on to his feet. "Please don't call me," he says.

"What?"

"Just leave me alone. For a while. Please." He lifts his hand in a kind of farewell and turns away.

"What about your things at the café?"

"I'll get them another time."

"Simon!"

He walks, shoulders up, tense. . . Simon — my best friend. My only friend.

I kick a bollard, kick it again and again and again.

"That's enough of that, young lady," says an elderly man as he passes me.

"Piss off," I say. He has the sense not to respond. Just shakes his head and walks on. He reminds me of my granddad. I hate myself even more and I walk back to the café alone.

"No luck?" says Cathy.

I burst into tears and she gives me a hug. That makes me cry even more. I'm glad there aren't any customers yet.

"Do you want to go home?" she says. "Have the day off?"

"No," I sniff. "I'd rather be busy and anyway, you can't manage by yourself."

"OK. Good. Let's get on with it then." She smiles and she doesn't ask any questions.

I struggle my way through the day. At the end of the afternoon, the phone rings and Cathy answers. I see her nod and hear her say, "Hang on, I'll just get her."

I experience a bubble of expectation. "Simon?" I mouth at her.

She turns her mouth down. "Your mum." She hands me the phone.

Mum sounds sensible and sober, but I can hear the strain in her voice as she tells me there are complications. They're having trouble keeping Gran stable. She's back in intensive care – Mum will be staying at the hospital and she'll update me in the morning. And NO, I definitely can't visit.

"But—"

"Not now, Amber, I've got to go."

The phone goes dead and I replace it slowly. I want to know if Gran has seen my card. I need to be sure she understands how sorry I am. She can't die without me saying sorry. She can't die full stop.

I polish the wooden tables, pressing the cloth hard into the surfaces and pushing it backwards and forwards, round and round. Next, I give the glass of the serving counter a good clean. I double-check for smears. I want to have it just as Gran would like it. Sparkling. I tell myself that if I don't leave any smears, then Gran will live. I check it about ten times. We're late closing because we have to cover all Simon's jobs too.

"He'll be back," says Cathy as we scrub down the kitchen.

"Not while I'm around, he won't," I say.

"Don't beat yourself up. You can't blame yourself for everything."

Cathy's wrong. I *can* blame myself. I do.

CHAPTER 11

By the time we leave, the sun of this morning has changed to drizzle and I chuck on a sweatshirt. Cathy locks up and I say goodbye, her setting off in one direction and me in the other. I don't hurry; all I've got waiting for me is an empty house.

Instinctively I reach for my phone – and then remember I haven't got one. I walk along in a miserable daze until I almost bump into someone and am forced to stop.

"Busy day?" The voice is husky and friendly. I look up and a warmth fills my chest.

"Tyler! What is it with you and surprising me?" I try to sound normal but my heart is skittering.

"I've been in town," he says.

"And you just happened to be hanging out near the café?"

"Sort of." He falls into step beside me.

"Are you stalking me?" I give him a playful nudge.

"How else do I get hold of you?"

I can feel the pink spreading from my neck to my face.

"Do you mind?" he asks.

Do I mind? Right now I could fling my arms round him. He's the only person that seems to want to be with me.

"You look a bit done in," he says. "How's your gran?"

"Not great. Mum's with her. She doesn't want to see me."

"Your gran or your mum?"

"Both probably."

Tyler puts his arm round my shoulders, giving me a reassuring hug. "I don't think I could ever go back to that hospital," he says. "Maybe they're just trying to make things easier for you."

"Yeah, right."

He gives a final squeeze and drops his arm back to his side and we walk on in silence for a few paces. Then he says, "I've got something for you."

"You have?"

"I found your phone."

136

I stop walking. "How come?"

He taps his nose twice.

"I don't believe you," I say and he grins. "Go on then, hand it over."

"I haven't got it with me. It's back at the caravan. That's why I wanted to catch you – so you can come back with me and pick it up."

I smile. His plan is not exactly subtle. "Did you check it? Is it working?"

"Yep, good as new."

I puff out air. "Well that's a bit of luck."

He slips his hand into mine and I don't stop him. As we walk, his grip on my hand becomes more insistent. "So you'll come with me then?"

"What, now?"

"Why not?"

I pause and shake my head. "I want to – I really do. It's just with Gran and everything. I think I have to play by the rules for a while."

"I thought rules were made to be broken," he says with a dry laugh. "That's what Liam used to say."

"Did he?" I never noticed him breaking any. I think I've broken enough for a lifetime over the last few days.

Tyler's eyes wander away from mine and I follow

his gaze to a small group of people huddled against a wall between two shops.

"Are you OK?" I say.

"Yeah – fine." He drags his eyes back to me and we walk towards a bench and sit down.

"Come on, Amber. Please come. I thought you said you wanted to see me again." He touches my cheek with the back of his hand – the same as he did yesterday. Any resistance I had begins to melt away and I know I don't need much persuading. Mum's at the hospital. Dad won't be back. What's stopping me? Tyler puts his finger on my chin and strokes it down my neck to my chest.

"I'm not wearing it," I say. "It's in my bag."

"I like it when you wear it."

"No one knows I've got it apart from you. I can't risk wearing it with Mum and Dad around."

"Our secret." He smiles, leans in towards me and gives me the lightest kiss on the lips. Tiny bubbles of happiness fizz around my body. I like that my secret is shared; I like Tyler. "Don't worry, I won't tell anyone," he says and he kisses me again. Gentle – not demanding.

My body responds with an impulsive rush of anticipation, a thrill of the unknown as my world shrinks down to just Tyler and me. But he pulls away and I wonder if I've done something wrong. His focus has switched back to the group. They are watching us, I'm sure of it and I'm suddenly embarrassed and self-conscious.

"Do you know them?" I ask.

"Yeah. They're mates. I think they'd like to meet you. I've told them all about you," he says.

I feel a rush of pride mixed with disappointment. Tyler is telling his friends about me. They want to meet me. But why are they hanging around right now? Would Tyler rather spend time with them? Something doesn't feel right.

"Come on," he says. I try to fight my shyness. If these are his friends then I need to make a good impression.

Tyler leads me towards them. As we approach, he grips my hand a little tighter.

"This is Amber," he says. "Declan, Joel, Becky." He nods at each one in turn.

"Hi," I say uncertainly.

They size me up – literally stare me up and down. I swallow. The one called Declan raises his eyebrows very slightly and says, "Nice to meet you. How's it going?" He doesn't wait for a reply. He turns to the others. "So I'll see you back at the caravan then – in thirty?"

"Is *she* coming?" asks the girl.

"Of course she is," says Declan.

The fizz, the thrill and the anticipation have gone and I curl back into myself. I want it to be just me and Tyler.

"Actually, I should go home," I say. "I'm kind of grounded at the moment."

"Grounded?" says Declan with mock horror. "That is terrible. And what will Mummy and Daddy do to you if you don't go home?"

They all laugh. I feel stupid so I laugh too. "I guess they won't do much – they're not there."

Declan wipes his forehead dramatically. "Phew! Grounded by absent parents; made me sweat to think about it."

There's more laughter and Tyler puts his arm around me again. We start walking, me between Declan and Tyler.

"Has she been to your caravan before?" Becky asks.

"Yes, she has," says Tyler.

"I was there on Saturday night, since you ask," I say pointedly.

Declan chuckles, licks the tip of his finger and

draws an imaginary line in the air. Becky looks fed up and Joel gives a snort, or is it a laugh? Clearly, I'm excluded from this little joke. I glance at Tyler but his eyes are on the ground. We head into a car park, threading our way through the lines of cars. I walk almost in a trance.

"I'll meet you there," says Declan to no one in particular, as he opens the door of the car next to Tyler's. "I've got a couple of things to sort."

"I'll come with you," says Becky and takes a couple of steps towards Declan's car. Declan blocks her.

"No. You go with Tyler. You can look after Amber."

"I'm not bloody well—"

"Quit your jabbering. Just keep your mouth shut, OK?" Declan is only centimetres away from Becky and they're eyeball to eyeball.

Becky pouts and looks at her feet. Declan stands absolutely still until she lifts her head again. He points a finger against her chest. Everyone is silent, watching. Declan doesn't say a word, just gives her a small push, swings himself into the driver's seat and slams the door. He starts the car, revs it hard and drives away leaving behind a tense silence. We get into Tyler's car, Becky and me in the back, Tyler and Joel in the front. Becky looks upset. I should try to be nice.

"Are you all right?" I say.

Becky angles her body away from me. "None of your business. Just because—"

"You heard what Declan said," Joel says, turning round and looking at Becky. "Keep your mouth shut."

"You can shut up yourself." Becky crosses her arms and sits back hard against the seat.

I catch Tyler's warning glance in the rear-view mirror. He hits the volume on the radio and cranks up the music; a loud bass beat thumps through the car. No one speaks and Becky stares out of the window with a face like thunder.

There's a build-up of traffic as we head out of the city centre and Joel reckons he knows a good shortcut. It's a smart area of town – big houses with neat gardens.

"Slick Street," says Becky in a disinterested voice.

"Shut it!" says Joel, shaking his head. Becky gives the back of his seat a kick.

We drive on and stop at some random place to pick up pizzas. Tyler collects money from the others but he won't take mine. He says it's his shout.

I try to insist. I got plenty of tips this morning, but he won't take anything.

Left in the car with Joel and Becky, the atmosphere is hardly friendly. Joel asks me a series of predictable questions, but he's too busy playing games on his phone to listen to the answers.

"How long have you been working at the café?" he says.

How does he know I work at the café? "A couple of years. Have you been in?"

He shakes his head. "Nah. Don't do cafés. Do you like it?"

"Yeah, it's fine."

His fingers work the buttons on his phone. "Can you make that fancy coffee?"

Becky jabs her finger into the back of his head. "As if you'd know anything about fancy coffee."

They start sniping away at each other and Joel turns up the volume on his phone, pretending to completely ignore her. Eventually Becky gives up and goes back to staring out of the window. By the time Tyler emerges with pizza boxes piled on his forearms, I'm about ready to get out of the car and walk home. Seeing his smile changes all that and I get out to give him a hand.

"Thanks," he says and rolls his eyes at the others.

"Well trained," says Becky once I'm back in the car, as she continues to stare out of the opposite window.

The pizzas are warm on my lap and, as we set off down the smaller, winding lanes, the rich cheesy smell makes me feel carsick.

We pull up at the entrance to the paddock and Joel opens the gate.

"Don't wait," says Becky, getting out and joining him. "Joel and I are going to take a walk." She stands and watches with her arms crossed as Joel struggles to close it again.

"Slow Joe," says Tyler and grins at me.

"Are him and Becky together?"

"On and off. They break up about once a week and then make up again. It's stupid. Joel's not the cleverest and Becky runs rings round him."

I decide it's best to keep my thoughts about Becky to myself.

We drive through the yard, leaving the other two behind. This time, I take in my surroundings properly. Not that they're exactly memorable. The yard is full of stripped-out old cars, battered furniture and no end of other stuff.

"Not pretty, is it?" says Tyler. His body language has softened now it's only us in the car. "I like it, though. It's a place I can disappear."

I look at the piles of unwanted junk. "Do you want to disappear?"

He shrugs. "Don't you?"

I consider this for a moment. "Most of the time, I think I already have. People only seem to notice I exist when there's trouble."

"I notice you exist."

I know I'm blushing again. The warmth in my face matches the warmth inside my chest, my stomach, my everywhere.

Tyler parks the car and we get out – it's good to be in the fresh air. I help carry the pizzas to the caravan, then Tyler closes the door behind us and takes the boxes from me, putting them on the side.

We stand close to each other – too close to be comfortable without touching. He seems uncertain. I'm unwilling to make the first move. He scratches his fingers backwards and forwards through his hair, making it stand up in spikes. I laugh.

"You didn't believe me about your phone, did you?" he says. He turns around and searches in a small drawer before pulling it out. "I wasn't lying and I've even charged it for you. Sonia's got the same one, luckily."

"Thank you." I hold out my hand but he doesn't give it to me.

"You've got plenty of messages," he says, holding the phone against his chest.

"How would you know?"

"I had to check the phone was working, didn't I? I haven't read them."

"Of course you haven't." I hold out my hand more insistently.

"Are you sure Simon isn't your boyfriend?" he asks.

"I thought you just said you didn't read them."

He folds his arms, trapping my phone underneath them.

"Well?" he says.

"Simon's a good friend. That's all." As I say it, I wonder if I can even describe him as that any more.

"That's good." Tyler looks thoughtful, then places my phone in my hand and holds it there, so it's sandwiched between our two hands, our fingers touching. He doesn't let go. His eyes hold mine, blue to brown. Not for the first time, there's something in the stillness of that gaze that unsettles me; as if he sees me, but doesn't see me. He doesn't move and doesn't speak. Finally he lets go of the phone and steps away. I don't trust myself to move.

"Did Kelly and Simon know each other before?" Tyler asks.

"Sorry?"

"Your friend Simon – did Kelly know him before the party the other night?"

I frown. "Not really. She might've met him with me a while back. Why?"

Tyler shrugs. "Just wondered. Anyway, he's left you a heap of messages." He nods towards the phone.

I switch it on and flick through the messages. His eyes don't leave me. I don't need to look up, I just know. He watches as my life unravels. Text after text from Simon on the night of Kelly's party.

On my way. Be there shortly.

R U OK?

At front door. Where R U?

Now in kitchen. Trying to ring. Answer your phone.

I keep scrolling down. The story of that night.

Someone said u left. Where are you?

Answer your phone.

To pisedd to drive.

Fk u.

Messages from Gran, Gran, Gran, Gran, Mum, Dad, Dad. Frantic messages about where I am and what I'm doing. Each text yells at me louder than the last. Then more from Simon.

URGENT. Contact me or your parents.

Your Gran is in hospital. ANSWER YOUR PHONE

There are a couple more messages from Simon. Yesterday.

Can you meet me? We need to talk.

Please.

I wish I'd got those last messages. Maybe I could have managed things better between us. Too late now.

I don't dare listen to the voice messages. I don't want to hear Simon, Mum, Dad or, worst of all, Gran. If she dies, her voice will be on my phone and everything she says will remind me of what I did. What would Gran's last message say? *I can't believe you've done this to me, Amber?* I picture her collapsing on her pathway.

My knees don't want to hold me up any more. Gently, Tyler takes my phone and switches it off, then wraps his arms around me and strokes my hair. It reminds me of the way Liam used to comfort me when I was younger. I feel safe – I feel cared for.

Voices approach the caravan. Tyler doesn't let go. He kisses me gently on the forehead and keeps hold of me, rocking me slowly backwards and forwards.

"Oooh! Sorry for interrupting," says Becky as the door bangs open.

"Shut up," says Tyler.

"Tetchy," she says.

He doesn't let go of me. I'm embarrassed and I press him away, tucking my hair behind my ears. I don't want Becky and Joel here.

"Come on, Ty, the pizza's getting cold," says Joel. "And some of us have worked up a bit of an appetite." He pulls Becky into the caravan. She giggles and nudges him.

A change seems to come over Tyler. His face hardens and his hands pump as if he's squeezing something in his fists. Joel and Becky bring the boxes over to the table and start opening them. The pizza is still vaguely warm –Tyler rips off a slice and holds it out to me.

"Eat," he says.

We sit, eat, talk. The food gives me energy. I begin to feel better and start to relax. Tyler sits close to me. Becky and Joel watch us. Becky's still ignoring me, but she's more chilled and she starts telling stories about her mum and her mum's boyfriend. He moved into the house six months ago with his two young kids and now he thinks he runs the place. Her mum does what she's told. The boyfriend doesn't want Becky around. He's said that straight to her face. He doesn't like her friends either. Apparently, on Saturday, Becky turned up with Joel and the boyfriend threw them both out. Becky says she's never going back. She looks at me as if to say *beat that*, then carries on talking to the boys.

"And what's more," she says, waving a slice of pizza in the air, "now mum's complaining because she hasn't got anyone to babysit the kids. She should've thought of that before – it's her tough luck."

Then Joel launches in and starts talking about his dad's drinking and how it's best not to be around when he's drunk. I nod in agreement. The way they tell it makes it all sound unimportant, but every now and again their eyes betray them. This is not what life is supposed to be like, but we're all stuck in it and we have to get on with it. That's the message. Listening to them and realizing I'm not the only one putting up with stuff at home is a good feeling. I wonder how much Tyler has told them about me. I notice he hasn't opened his mouth once.

We keep eating until all that's left are some ragged crusts and the pineapple that Tyler's picked off. Joel chucks the boxes outside the caravan. Tyler picks up his guitar and starts to strum. He rests one foot on the table and props his guitar on his bent leg, his body relaxed back against a pillow. I follow the line of his slim arms as they stretch from the sleeves of his baggy T-shirt. The fingers of his left hand move up and down the guitar while the other hand gently plucks the strings. I'd like to slide into the gap between his guitar and his body and stay there.

"Shall I do your nails?" asks Becky, leaning across the table and taking my hand. Her sudden attention takes me by surprise.

I look down at my bitten nails, the ragged cuticles. "Not much point," I say.

"Yeah, there is. Come on. Stick your hands over here."

Becky fiddles in a bag. Pulls out nail varnish. My eyes keep straying back to Tyler and he smiles. Becky brushes electric blue on to my nails.

"Interesting choice of colour," says Joel. "Unless Amber's a Chelsea supporter. Now that wouldn't please Declan."

"Don't be such a tosser," says Becky. "It's nail varnish. What do you want me to do, paint them in red and white stripes?" I note that Becky's nails are bright red.

"My dad would lynch me if I supported Chelsea," I say.

Tyler presses his lips together and I know we're both thinking the same thing. All the football stuff in Liam's room. Liam playing the dedicated Saints supporter to keep Dad happy. Tyler shifts his foot so it's resting against mine and strums something more energetic and upbeat. Liam is a secret bond between us; a bond that no one else can share. It doesn't matter about the others. I shake my hands to dry the nail varnish then blow on it gently. I wonder if Liam hung out with Tyler like this. I wonder if they came here?

The sound of a car bumping over the yard stops everything. Tyler and Joel exchange glances. Tyler stops playing and slides his guitar back into the cupboard. Becky puts away the nail varnish and goes into the toilet. There's nothing laid-back about the atmosphere now.

When Becky comes out, she's got lipstick on and one of the buttons on her shirt is undone so her bra is showing. Should I tell her? A car door bangs, then Declan appears in the doorway of the caravan. He's not large, yet his presence makes the caravan seem small and claustrophobic. Becky moves close to Declan and he flicks her hair with his fingers.

"Take Amber out for a walk, will you?" he says.

Becky presses herself against him as she moves towards the door and whispers something in his ear. Her body language is so obvious that Joel can't have missed it. Declan makes a small head movement in my direction and Tyler shifts to let me out.

"Why do I have to go for a walk?" I say. Becky looks at me with an expression somewhere between boredom and disgust.

"It's OK, babe," Tyler says smoothly. "It won't be for long."

Babe? Since when did Tyler start calling me babe? I resist as Tyler pushes me up. "Do this for me," he whispers. He stands up behind me and his arms circle my waist, his hands resting gently on my hip bones.

Declan watches me closely. I turn my head so I can see Tyler's face. I question him silently. He hardly looks at me but I see a flash of something. Fear?

"Here." He lets go of me and slips off his hoodie. "It may not be so warm out there now, take this."

"Aren't we the gentleman," says Becky.

I narrow my eyes at her and she doesn't react at all.

Tyler presses me towards the door where Becky is waiting.

"This way," says Becky. "I'll take you to the barn."

Declan smiles at her and winks. Gran says never to trust a man who winks.

After the warmth in the caravan, the air is cool and I'm grateful for the hoodie. It smells faintly of pizza, strongly of cigarettes and unmistakably of Tyler. I hug it around me as we follow the path down the side of the hedge and keep going.

"Why did Declan ask you to take me for a walk?" I ask. I may as well try to make conversation.

"Boy stuff," she says.

"Boy stuff like what?"

"How would I know? I'm just a girl." The way she says it is suddenly angry.

"What's with you and Declan, anyway?"

"What do you mean?"

"Well there's obviously something going on."

"It's complicated," she says twiddling the button of her shirt. "Hands off, though."

"But I thought you were going out with Joel. . . ?"

Becky flashes me a shut-up look and I shrug. Why would I be interested in Declan anyway? I only met him like a couple of hours ago. It must be pretty clear that Tyler and me are. . . I frown. What are we? Anyway, Becky needn't worry.

The further we get from the caravan, the more relaxed Becky becomes. The smells and sounds are different out here in the countryside and the sky is turning a gold-edged pink. You can almost see her softening.

"Red sky at night, shepherd's delight," she says. "No idea what that's supposed to mean but my nan always used to say it."

"Is she still alive?"

"No. Died a few years back. Yours?"

"She's in hospital."

"Oh. I'm sorry. Shame."

Shame. That about sums up the way I feel. I consider telling Becky about it, but I'm not sure of her yet. We keep walking for a few minutes until we reach a corrugated-iron building, which must be the barn. The whole place smells abandoned, unwanted, neglected. Inside, blackened straw bales have been pushed around to make a kind of seating area. Becky plonks herself down on one and the dust rises in a great puff, catching in my throat and making me cough.

She starts to roll herself a cigarette, then offers the tobacco to me.

I shake my head and she smiles.

"Go on," she says. "One won't hurt you."

"I can't. It's not good for my running." Training has always been a useful excuse for not smoking.

"Running?"

"Yeah. Cross country and long distance mainly."

Becky runs her tongue along the paper and sticks it down. "What do you want to do that for? What's the point?"

It's a good question.

She flicks her lighter and holds it to the end of her cigarette. Once it's lit she holds it out to me. "Sure?" she asks.

I don't want to be lame, so I take it and try to take a puff without inhaling. She laughs and I hand it back to her.

"Is that safe in here?" I stare around at all the straw.

"Probably not." She inhales deeply and reaches behind the straw bale, pulling out an old mug. It's already stuffed full of cigarette butts. "So how long have you known Tyler?"

"About three years," I answer.

"That long?" She seems surprised. "How come you've not been round before?"

"We haven't hung out together in a while. I'm more a friend of Kelly's."

"Kelly?"

"Tyler's sister. Or stepsister. Tyler was friends with my brother."

"Was? What happened — did they fall out or something?"

Little goosebumps press at my skin. I had the impression Becky and Tyler knew each other pretty well.

"My brother died."

"No shit!"

Her reaction is, at least, different and it makes me smile. But the fact Tyler's said nothing strikes me as odd. You'd have thought he'd have mentioned Liam, at least. I decide to steer the conversation away from me and Liam.

"How about you?" I ask. "How long have you known Tyler for?"

"I don't know. About eight months, maybe. Under a year, anyway."

She finishes her cigarette, stubs it out in the mug. She flops back against the straw and closes her eyes. I hug my knees up inside Tyler's sweatshirt and listen to the silence of the barn, but my mind isn't silent at all. Perhaps Tyler is trying to create some kind of new life for himself with people who know nothing about him or his past. But if that's the case, why is he hanging out with me? The longer we sit here, the colder I get. Becky seems to be asleep. The straw prickles through my jeans.

A sharp whistle sounds in the distance. Becky opens her eyes and sits up, immediately alert.

"You can go back now," she says.

"How come?"

"That's what Declan's whistle means."

"He whistles and we're expected to move? Like dogs?"

"He's OK." Becky flops forward and stares at the ground, her elbows on her knees. "You'll get used to it. You'd better go."

"What about you?"

"I'll hang around here for a while." She looks up at me and smiles. It's hard to read her expression. I hesitate, but she's already busy rolling another cigarette. "Go on," she says waving me away, "and tell Declan to bring a blanket, will you? I'm fed up of this prickly straw."

I retrace my footsteps to the caravan. The sky has now turned deep red and the last light is fading fast. I'm trying to work out the Declan, Becky, Joel triangle. It's weird.

When I get to the caravan, I'm not sure what to do. I put my ear to the door and listen. "You'd better not be pissing me about," I hear Declan say. Do I knock? I decide not and open the door slowly. Three faces turn towards me and the talking stops.

"Becky said to come back," I say.

"Glad to hear she's teaching you the ropes," says Declan.

"Where is she?" asks Joel.

"She said to take a blanket," I say quietly, to no one in particular.

Declan cleans his nails with a pocket knife. "Come on, Joel, don't look so hard done by. You know the deal," he says.

"Yeah, I know the deal." Joel's voice is flat, resigned.

Whatever the deal is, it's clear Joel doesn't like it. I look towards Tyler, but he's watching Joel too.

As I move to sit down, Declan stands up and blocks my way. I widen my eyes at him, not understanding. "Your turn next," he says and his hand brushes against my chest and rests there for a few seconds. His meaning is clear. I try to wriggle round him and his eyes lock on to mine, eyebrows slightly raised. I don't let my gaze leave his. I take a step towards him, slightly sideways and tread as hard as I can on his foot, pressing hard, eye to eye. I know it's hurting and I know it's a mistake. He doesn't react, at least not outwardly, but the challenge in his eyes turns to something cold and hard. He removes his foot from under mine, turns and walks out.

I sit down next to Tyler. I'm not sure he saw what happened, not really.

I know I've made myself an enemy.

CHAPTER 12

It's getting late and the light is fading. I want out of here before Declan gets back. I prefer Tyler when he's not with his mates. Joel's splayed out, morose, across one of the seats, munching his way through a bag of jelly babies. The smell is sickly, the sound worse. Tyler reaches for his guitar again and seems keen to avoid eye contact or conversation. I check my watch.

"I need to be getting home soon," I say.

Tyler keeps playing, as if he hasn't heard me, then suddenly makes an aggressive strum of his fingers across the strings of his guitar and pushes it to one side.

"We can't leave yet," he says. "Why don't you ring your mum and find out how it's going at the hospital. If everything's OK, then what's the problem with staying?" His tone is almost harsh.

Joel stops chewing and watches us.

"No, I have to get back. I told you earlier."

Tyler raises a shoulder. "Yeah – but still – what's the rush?"

"If you must know, I don't much want to stay here with Declan around."

Tyler looks nervously at Joel. "Declan's all right," he says.

"Declan's a dick." I notice their anxious glances towards the door. "Oh, come on, it's not as if he's going to hear. He's too busy with Becky." I aim my last comment in Joel's direction and he stares into his near-empty bag of sweets.

"It's not what you think," says Tyler.

I sigh loudly. All I want is to be alone with Tyler. When he's with this lot he behaves like a dick too.

"Please take me home," I say, taking his hand.

Tyler seems incapable of making a response. Instead he searches my eyes and I wonder if he's trying to pass me a silent message. I indicate with a nod of my head towards the door, that it would be a good idea to leave right now. Surely he can see it would be easier for us to talk if we were away from here? He doesn't move, just puts one hand on my leg as if to hold me in place. I stand up, frustrated, and walk out – straight into Declan.

"Going somewhere?" he asks.

I grip the doorway of the caravan. "Yes. Home."

"Oh, really? And how are you planning on getting there?"

"Tyler's taking me."

Declan looks around as if searching for Tyler and smiles. "No need to trouble Tyler. I'm going back into town. I can give you a ride." He makes it sound almost nice.

"Thanks, but don't worry. Tyler's already said he'll take me." I raise my voice to make sure Tyler hears.

"Shame," says Declan, cupping my chin in his hand so I have to look at him. "You don't know what you might be missing,"

I grab his wrist and pull his hand away.

He raises his eyebrows. I'm getting to recognize that look and to hate it. My heart pounds as I stand my ground.

Tyler's voice comes from behind me. "It's fine, I'm ready to take her."

Declan gives a small, tight smile. "Didn't you

164

hear?" he says, not taking his eyes off me, "I've just said, *I'll* take her."

Tyler steps down from the caravan. The tension ratchets up a few notches. Declan starts clicking his fingers repeatedly in a slow rhythm, as if waiting to see what Tyler's going to do.

"It was good to meet you," I say to Declan, trying to divert his attention. I move slowly backwards towards the car, my eyes on Declan all the way.

The air simmers. I can feel the head of his gaze.

Quick as a flash, Tyler is in the driver's seat. Declan laughs. "Next time then." His voice is like thick treacle. "Since your boyfriend seems so keen."

I get in beside Tyler and pull the door shut. I don't rush. I don't want Declan to see the panic inside.

Tyler starts the car and we leave, stopping only at the gate. He drives quickly and neither of us says a word. We're way along the lane before I drop my shoulders from my ears and let my head flop back.

"So," I say, "what was all that about?"

Tyler grips the steering wheel. "You shouldn't have wound him up, it's not a good idea."

"Me, wind *him* up?"

"It's just . . . you need to get to know him better."

"I don't want to get to know him better. How long have you known him for, anyway?"

"A while."

"And you're honestly telling me you like him?"

"He's a good mate. He's helped me out."

I'd like to ask what with, but I decide now is not the time.

"What were you doing when Becky and I were in the barn?"

"Nothing. Talking. You know."

The thing is, I don't know and I'd like to know.

"You're different when you're around him," I say.

"Yeah — well, it happens. You're different too."

The words trigger an echo in my head. The echo of a memory: of me telling Liam — shouting at Liam — that he was different when he was around Tyler. I chew the inside of my cheek.

"Did Liam know him?" I try to keep the question light.

In the long pause that follows, I watch Tyler's face. I can see a nerve working in his jaw, tiny pulsing movements.

"Tyler?" I push him for an answer, sit forward in my seat.

"No. Liam never met Declan."

I'm not sure I believe him. My imagination plays with possibilities. What if Liam had known Declan? I can't see them being friends. Maybe that's why he and Tyler were arguing. Maybe it's got something to do with what Liam was going to tell me.

I sigh. I'm being stupid.

"Declan's a bully." I say it as much to myself as to Tyler.

Tyler hardly speaks the rest of the way home. I've upset him, that's obvious, but I'll make it up to him when we get back to my place. I want to reach out and touch him, to make my peace. I do like him – I like him a lot. It's Declan I don't like.

We pull up outside the house.

"It's OK, no one's home," I say. "You can come in."

He shakes his head, not bothering to cut the ignition.

"Look, I'm sorry if I was out of order about Declan."

"Forget it. Just don't make trouble, that's all. Please."

I shrug. "So? Are you coming in or not?"

Tyler glances in the rear-view mirror. "I have to get going," he says. "Another time maybe."

I feel foolish and let down, but my mouth is working faster than my head.

"When will I see you?" I ask.

He glances behind him again, using the side mirror this time. I look back, but I can't see anything.

"I don't know. I don't think this is such a good idea."

I should get out, slam the door and walk, but brain and heart don't seem to be connected. So nothing happens at all. It's Tyler who breaks the silence.

"I'm sorry, Amber, I'm not very good at this. I'll come and get you from work tomorrow – no, not tomorrow, Wednesday. What time do you finish?"

He seems desperate to get away and I refuse to make a total fool of myself.

"Don't worry about it," I say. "It's not like you have to see me if you don't want to."

"I do want to. Wednesday. Tell me what time."

I search for clues in his face, something to prove

he's not just stringing me along.

"I'll be through by twelve. It's a half day."

"Fine," he says. "Twelve it is. I'll call you if anything changes."

"OK." I wait for him to lean over and kiss me goodbye, but he doesn't move. I get out and push the door shut. I want to feel happy. I want to believe I'll see him again.

I watch the red tail lights of his car until they're pin-pricks at the end of our road.

Only then do I realize I don't have his number. I've never given him my number so I don't know how he'll call me. Unless he took it from my phone.

With a growing sense of disappointment, I let myself into the house. In the darkness, the answerphone flashes. I flick on the lights and run through the messages. Most are from friends of Gran's and I save them.

Next message. 21.48. Monday, the automated voice of the system tells me. Not long ago. Dad's voice crackles over the machine.

"I thought I told you to stay at home. What part of the word grounded do you not understand? I'll be back tomorrow night. Mum is spending the night at the hospital. No mobiles allowed in intensive care so you won't be able to contact her. Oh – and they're hoping to have Gran back on high dependency in the next couple of days. If there's a bed."

I hate the way Dad updates me on Gran like an afterthought. Then there's another voice in the background. A woman's voice, it sounds like. Kind of teasing, seductive. Calling Dad's name. The message breaks off. I listen to it again. Who is Dad with at 9.48 on a Monday night?

I think of how often he's been away recently. I'm tempted to ring him. But that would be stupid. If I don't ring, I can tell him I was asleep when he called. He can't argue with that. I stare at the phone for a bit longer, wonder if Dad is sweating over his message. I listen to it again. I mustn't jump to conclusions. For a third time, I play it, and then press delete. I pick up my things and walk upstairs. Would anyone really fancy Dad?

I glance at Liam's door on the way past. What would he say about today, about Dad, about everything? I wander into my room, flop down on the bed and delve in my bag for Liam's stone. I want to feel the weight of it in my hands. I want to feel close to him. Except it's not in my bag. It's gone.

CHAPTER 13

Finders keepers, losers weepers. All night it sings in my head. Not sings exactly: chants – no, taunts, more like. In the irrational dark of half-sleep, I honestly believe that the stone has magical powers and, now it's gone, all my luck will desert me – like Liam's did him. I promised him I'd look after it, promised him I wouldn't lose it. I couldn't get it back to him on time. My dreams are terrible, breathless, frantic. Becky and Joel and Declan, but for some reason Declan is Dad.

I wake up sweating, with most of my duvet on the floor. It's early, not even seven. I empty my bag on the floor, feel through pockets, search downstairs, then upstairs. I was tired last night– I might've missed it.

Luck – dreams – Dad – Gran. I decide I should

ring Dad to tell him I was asleep when he called. Lies. My half-dreams stay with me and arriving at work without getting run over seems like a good result. I tell myself again and again that it's only a stone. Still, there's a tiny seed of doubt, enough to make me uneasy. I start to imagine pains in my chest.

It's a long day – a double shift to cover for Simon. A new guy, Josh, has started on trial and it's a pain supervising him as well as doing my own stuff. Luckily it's not too busy; the cold of the last few weeks has finally given way to proper summer and people are making the most of it. Josh gets the hang of things pretty quickly and he's good with the customers who do come in.

My mind is everywhere but on the job. I've backtracked through all my movements and the only place the stone can be is at Tyler's. I wish I could ring him, but I don't have his number. How stupid is that? Now I'll have to wait until tomorrow. My need to see Tyler has turned into something else – something vital and urgent.

I leave the café at 5.30 and head towards the supermarket. I have no idea what time Dad will be back or if I need to get food for Mum. Dad and Mum. I'd never given much thought to their relationship before – not until last night. Were they happy before Liam died? Do they love each other at all?

Someone brushes heavily against my side and a hand slides around my upper arm. I recognize the smell more than anything: a mixture of too much aftershave, cigarettes and sweat. Declan is beside me, propelling me along. So, they've decided to surprise me again after work, have they? I search around for Tyler.

"He's not here," says Declan, as if reading my mind.

"Where is he, then?"

"You think I'd bring your boyfriend along? That's not part of the deal."

"What deal? What are you doing here?"

"I've come to give you a lift home. To make up for yesterday."

The way he says it is heavy with meaning. I try to shake him off.

"I don't need a lift home, thanks."

"You might find you do. Have a little think about it." He tightens his hand around my arm. I'm strangely calm. I've been prepared for disaster all day and now it's here, it's almost comforting– like it was meant to be. Declan is bigger than me and much stronger. I drag back, slowing down the speed of his walk while I try to think.

"Dad will be at home. He's back this afternoon. I'm not allowed friends round at the moment."

"Is that right? We'll have to wait and see won't we? Sounds like a bit of a bully, your dad."

"It takes one to know one," I mutter. Declan gives a dry laugh and pinches my arm harder.

"I'm not like Becky, if that's what you think, so you can leave me alone."

"No, you're not, are you? That's what I like about you."

Towards the car park doors. . . I begin to believe he's serious; I begin to panic. I need to get away from him, but he's stronger than me by far. People avoid us; just another useless teenage couple having a row. Should I scream? Would anyone do anything then?

"Calm down," he hisses in my ear. "I'm giving you a lift home. Just trying to be helpful. That's ALL."

Think, Amber. Think.

We're nearly at the entrance. Once we're in

the car park, there'll be fewer people. I need to do something now.

A uniform. A half-familiar face. I manage to catch his eye. He looks at me and smiles.

"Amber! It is Amber isn't it?"

Declan's grip has already loosened. "See ya," he says, all friendly, and turns around, walking back the way we came.

The relief is overwhelming. My face is hot and flushed. I'm breathless.

"You probably don't remember me, it's PC Marsh."

I nod. I can't speak. I do remember him, of course I do.

"Sorry, I didn't mean to. . ." he says, looking over my shoulder. Declan has all but gone.

PC Marsh asks me how I'm doing.

"Good." My voice seems to struggle out through a fog.

"Hot, isn't it?" he says. "Not much going on in here today, I doubt."

He's jokey, friendly. I nod again. If only he knew.

He chats on for a bit longer, keeping the conversation vague, not mentioning Liam. "Well it's nice to see you," he finishes up. "Glad I bumped into you."

Not half as glad as I am, I think.

We say our goodbyes and as soon as I'm round the corner, I run. I run straight on to a waiting bus. It's not the right bus and it's going in the wrong direction, but I don't care. I need to get away from here, away from Declan. I wait for a couple of stops, then get off and take an alternative route home. What if Declan knows where I live? I should've said something to PC Marsh, but what? *This boy, who I know, is offering to give me a lift home and I don't trust him.* It was hardly going to result in instant arrest. What did I really think Declan was going to do? When I see Dad's car parked outside our house, I damn near celebrate. I never thought I'd be so pleased to see him.

"Dad?" I call, as soon as I'm in the door.

No answer. "Dad," I call again.

I hear a kind of grunt and find him in the sitting room, his laptop open on his knees. He raises his head and glances at his watch. "You're late," he says and goes back to tapping on the keyboard.

"Bus problems," I mumble as I try to blink back the tears. I so need a hug. I so need to talk to someone.

Suddenly life feels very complex and I don't know how to deal with it. I need Dad.

"There are some messages," I say, "on the machine. I deleted yours."

Dad looks at me for slightly too long and I wonder if we have an understanding.

He clears his throat. "I was working late," he says, putting his laptop to one side and standing up. I follow him out to the kitchen where he looks around. "I thought you said you'd pick up some food for tonight."

"I didn't get the chance. I. . ."

"Excuses, excuses. That's all it is with you. Anyway, I'm off to join Mum at the hospital. I'll get something there."

"No!" It comes out loud and desperate. "I mean, can't I come?"

"We've talked about this already."

"I know. But I could just sit in the waiting room."

"Don't be silly. If you're bored, I can find plenty to keep you occupied."

I stare up at the ceiling. I hate him. I hate Mum and Gran too. "Why won't she see me? I've said I'm sorry."

I trail behind him into the hall where he picks up

his wallet and keys.

"Dad. Please. Don't leave me alone tonight."

"Your mum needs me, Amber. You know that. It's hard for her supporting her mother through all this. A lot of stress."

I hang my head, the weight of blame sitting like a rock inside me. I hear him open the door, close it behind him and then I sit down on the bottom stair. The emptiness of the house threatens to swallow me up. I need help. I need support. *I* need intensive care.

But nobody notices.

For the second night in a row I am scared. I still haven't found the stone and tonight my fear has a shape and the shape is Declan.

CHAPTER 14

Twelve o'clock. I'm sure that's what we arranged. All morning, my stomach has been churning and I've been driving Cathy demented with my uselessness. 12.00 passes, then 12.15. Nervous humming turns to disappointment, frustration, then anger. By 12.30, it's obvious I've been stood up. Still, I don't leave the café because I have to see him. I *have* to see Tyler. I need to ask him about Liam's stone and I'm determined to find out what he knows about Declan's visit yesterday. Worse than that, I *want* to see him. I pretend I don't, but I do.

Last night I lay awake in the darkness until Dad arrived home. Thoughts of Tyler, Declan, Joel and Becky zigzagged in my head, making me restless and confused. I began to wonder if Declan's nastiness was in my imagination. Still I couldn't sleep until I knew Dad was back home and I wasn't alone. He dropped me at work again this morning and walked with me to the café – Mum had asked him to check everything was all right, apparently. He was checking up on me, more like, but today I was glad. Now I'm scared to leave the café by myself in case I'm jumped by Declan again. I check my phone a hundred times to see if there is a message from Tyler. I keep finding little jobs to delay leaving.

"What are you doing, Amber? It's your afternoon off. Go home!" Cathy smiles at me.

Outside, it's an airless, humid day and the material of my shirt sticks to my skin and seems to suck the energy out of me. On the spur of the moment, I send a text to Kelly. I don't know why I didn't think of it before.

Tyler's number? Have left something at his place.

Her answer pings back straight away.

Sorry don't have it. BTW nice seeing Simon again!

Don't have it? I close my eyes and shake my head. He must've told her not to give it to me. I read the message again. Seeing Simon's name makes things worse still. This is stupid. Life is stupid. All of it. I take a deep breath and march out of the café to the bus stop. My eyes are everywhere, wanting to find Tyler, not wanting to see Declan. All the way home, I keep a lookout for Tyler's car, but I know I'm grasping at straws. I rub my neck, where the stone should be. Seems the luck has well and truly run out. I try to be sensible and grown-up. I won't let myself cry, however desperate I feel.

The house is a sauna and I fling the windows wide open. It makes no difference, there's not even a hint of a breeze. Everything happens in slow motion when you're miserable and hot. Minutes stretch out with nothing to fill them. Sounds are dampened. I decide a cool shower is the only answer, though even that takes enormous effort. A cool shower then I'll lie on my bed. Perhaps I'll sleep. It's as good a plan as any. I can't think of anything else to do.

In the bathroom, I peel the clothes from my skin and chuck them in a limp pile in the corner. The water is shockingly cold, tingling, almost numbing. I force myself to stand under it until I'm shivering.

Bloody Tyler.

As I step out, the phone starts ringing. I grab my towel, fling it round me and run downstairs. I pick up. "Hello." Please let it be him. "Hello?" There's silence at the other end.

"Hello-o?" I say a final time. It must be a hoax call or Mum trying to call from the hospital with a dodgy signal. I give it another couple of seconds, my sopping wet hair dripping on to the phone and making a small puddle on the floor. I wipe the phone against my towel and put it down. I guess whoever it was will probably ring again in a minute, so I wander into the kitchen.

I don't get it at first – I can't actually believe what I'm seeing. Then I full-on freak out. Tyler is there with Declan and Joel – all three of them standing in my kitchen.

"*What* are you doing? How did you get in here?" I'm furious and embarrassed, conscious of my dripping hair and my nakedness under the towel.

They hardly react at all – except the way Declan looks at me makes me pull my towel tighter. He nods towards the window. "You need to take care with leaving windows open."

"Like it's normal to climb in people's windows? Most people ring the doorbell." I don't try to hide my anger. My heart is almost busting out of my ribcage.

"We only did it for a laugh," says Tyler.

"Well it's not funny."

"I said I'd see you after work."

"You said you'd pick me up *from* work, actually."

"Did I?"

"Alone," I add, though I'm not sure we ever discussed this.

"Well, I've come to pick you up now."

Declan flips his phone from one hand to the other and I have a strong suspicion it was him who made the call, that they've been spying on me, that this is all staged in some way. I do not want Declan in my kitchen. I don't want him anywhere near me.

Declan and Joel lounge against the kitchen sides as if they own the place and I'm the intruder. I want to tell them to get out. Tyler hovers, as if unsure what to do.

"Aren't you going to offer us a drink?" asks Declan.

"No. I'm going upstairs to put some clothes on."

"How disappointing." I'm not sure if he means the drink or the clothes, but either way I loathe him more than ever.

"And, in the meantime, you can all leave. Tyler will show you where to find the door. It's so much easier to use than a window."

"Very witty," says Declan and he starts opening cupboards until he finds a glass, then pours himself some water. He raises his glass to me and drinks it down.

I catch Tyler's eye, but he won't hold mine. "We're going to the park. We thought you'd like to come with us," he mumbles.

We? I don't like this *we*. "I don't feel like going to the park. It's too hot."

"Oooh. I don't feel like going to the park," Declan parrots back at me. "Will Daddy be home soon to check up on you?"

Blood rushes to my cheeks and I hate myself for it.

"And Becky's sick," says Joel, "so we need your help."

"Becky?" I look at all three of them in turn. Joel looks awkward and Tyler looks anywhere but me, so I let my gaze rest on Declan. "What's wrong with

Becky?"

"A bad cold," he says.

"And you need my help for a bad cold?"

Declan laughs. "That's funny, that's really funny." He hoists himself up so he's sitting next to the sink. "We don't need your help looking after Becky. We need you to come and take her place, so to speak."

"Are you kidding me?" An image of Becky with her button undone comes into my head. The memory of Declan yesterday. I pull my towel tighter still. Not me. I'm not going there.

I think Tyler must read my thoughts. "We need an extra pair of hands, that's all. It's not much." I sense he's trying to keep his voice gentle and relaxed. He's doing a good job of hiding the tension — but not quite good enough.

"What for?" I ask.

Declan folds his arms and smiles. "You've proved you're a girl who knows her own mind. Don't you think it's time you showed your parents they can't push you around? It's your life. That's why we'd like you to join us."

His eyes challenge and dare me at the same time.

"Join you?" I say. I just need to buy time while I

work out what to do.

"Come on," says Joel. "It's a lovely day."

I don't like the way Declan is looking at me. Does Tyler know, I wonder? About yesterday?

"I thought we had a date," I say to Tyler. "Standing in for Becky isn't exactly what I had in mind."

Tyler doesn't respond and the atmosphere in the kitchen has changed.

Declan's drawn himself up on the side so he's sitting very tall and he leans forward slightly – overbearing and overpowering. "We're not asking you to come," he says, "we're telling you. It's not an option. Now be a good girl and do as you're told." His voice is threatening; everything about him is threatening.

"Fuck off," I say. I know it's a mistake before the words hit the air.

Tyler takes my hand and flashes me a warning glance, but Declan's already jumped down. He comes right up to me, his face too close to mine. I've got my back to the wall and there's nowhere else to go. The cold brick presses against my shoulder blades. He hooks his finger over the top of my towel and I can feel his knuckle against my breastbone.

If he pulls now, my towel will come off and I'll be left naked. I keep my face turned away from his, avoiding eye contact. I can feel his breath against my face. Minty. Sweet.

"You'll do as you're told and you'll keep that mouth of yours shut. Do you understand?"

I do understand. I understand he's threatening me. I understand I have to do what they ask because there's one of me and three of them. My towel is coming loose and the only thing keeping it around me is the pressure from my biceps.

"Let go of me," I say. "Please."

"There's no point in trying to run," he says. "We know where you live and where you work. In fact, we know most things about you."

"Why are you doing this to me?" I ask.

"Perhaps you should've been a little more cooperative yesterday," he hisses right into my ear.

Tyler must've known. His lips are pressed together and he's staring at the floor. I can see his fists clenching and unclenching. Have I misjudged him that badly? *Do something*, I plead with him silently. *Don't just stand there.* A momentary flick of his eyes towards me and I can see he's as scared as I am.

"How touching," sneers Declan. "Looking at

your boyfriend for help. Save yourself the bother, I think you'll find his loyalty is with me, isn't it Tyler?"

"I don't have to do anything you say." My voice comes out cracked and husky. "Get out of my house."

Declan lets go of me with a sharp shove and pulls something from his pocket. I shrink back, expecting him to pull a knife. Instead, dangling in front of my eyes, is Liam's stone. Declan, his back to the window, holds it high in the air, where it swings slowly, catching the light from the sun. Something explodes inside my chest and I have to grit my teeth to hold it in. I can't take my eyes from the stone. Liam's stone in Declan's hands.

"We know all about Liam – don't we, Tyler?" says Declan.

Declan knows nothing about Liam. That's what Tyler told me. He said Liam never knew Declan. Someone is lying. The stone hangs just out of my reach. I can't control myself and I lunge for it.

"Not so fast," says Declan, tossing it over his head at Joel who catches it.

"How did you get it?" I shout.

"Shut up and go and get dressed." He grabs my

arm and twists it.

I close my eyes against the pain and the fear.

"I'll come," I say. "I'll come."

"Of course you will," he says in an oh-so-pleasant voice. "Now go and get ready."

Tyler is immediately by my side, his hand pressing against my back, gently pushing me towards the stairs. My brain is sending messages to my legs to move, but my legs aren't responding.

"It's all right," he whispers, increasing the pressure, keeping me moving.

He follows me all the way up and into my room where he closes the door and leans hard against it.

I put as much space between us as possible. Hate is an easy emotion to deal with. I hate Declan and I should hate Tyler. I want to hate him.

"I'm sorry," he says.

"Did you bring them here? Was it your idea?"

He shakes his head.

"Did you steal Liam's stone from me?"

He pauses. "Not exactly."

"You've got to tell me what this is about."

Tyler looks lost, agonizingly lost. I can't hate him. My instinct is to wrap my arms around him and protect him, but I force myself to keep a distance between us.

"What did Declan mean about yesterday?" he asks.

"You don't know?" I open my cupboard and try to find clothes. I need simple actions, little tasks to calm me down. "He was waiting for me. After work."

Tyler is shaking his head. "And?"

"He offered to give me a lift home." My stomach contracts as I say it, as if I'm going to throw up. The thought of what might have been. I push it from my mind.

Tyler takes a ragged breath in, tips his head back and flattens his hands against his cheeks and pulling the skin downwards, away from his eyes.

"Look, cooperate today, and perhaps that will be the end of it," he says.

"The end of what?"

"It's complicated. Just do this for me, will you?"

"It would help if I knew what it is I'm doing. I don't understand what's going on here."

"Come *on* Amber, it's nothing."

The way he says it makes me doubt him even more.

"You heard Declan. He was threatening me. Why would he threaten me if it's nothing? Tell me what he meant about knowing all about Liam. How did he get my stone?"

"Liam's stone."

I shriek with frustration. "Liam is dead. It's the only thing I have of his. You know that. You have to get it back. I promised. . ."

Tyler pulls at his hoodie. He must be baking. "We'll get it back. Do as Declan tells you – just this once – then they'll leave off bothering you. And me, come to that."

"And if I don't?"

"Please, Amber. It's not worth going against him. It's fine. I promise it won't happen again."

I look at my arm. The marks where Declan gripped me are still there. I try to ignore my emotions, try to keep my thoughts on track.

"You need to get ready," he says, his hand on the door. I wait for him to leave, but he doesn't. It's as if he's trying to make up his mind what to do. I listen to his unsteady breathing. Suddenly he comes towards me. I place my balled fists against his chest, holding him away.

"We need to stick together." He says each word

slowly, with emphasis. "And Declan's right. It's time you stopped being pushed around by your parents. We'll look after you."

"I don't need looking after," I say. "I'm quite capable of looking after myself."

Tyler nods slowly, then turns and leaves the room.

CHAPTER 15

Tyler's battered car creaks under the weight of the four of us: Joel and me in the back, the others in the front. Joel's got an old football on his lap and he's drumming on it with his fingertips in a steady monotonous rhythm. I'd like to pull his hands away and pin them to the seat. Declan's driving and I notice he's angled the rear-view mirror so that he has a clear reflection of me. I have to look away so we don't make eye contact. There's a strong smell of sweat and I angle my head towards the open window and breathe the fresh air.

We stop off at the local Spar and Tyler's sent in to buy beers. He comes out with two six-packs which he puts on the floor in front of him. We continue driving until we reach a nicer area of town. We leave the car and walk a random route to a small park. I don't know why we couldn't bring the car closer, especially in this heat.

The boys kick around the football for a while, in a bored kind of way. I try to join in, but I'm not in the mood for running around and I'm pretty useless so I give up and flop down on the grass. They soon join me. It all feels like a bit of a facade. Beers are handed out and I listen to the click and hiss of ring pulls being opened. Declan opens another and presses it into my hand. I don't like beer, but I know better now than to try and cross Declan. I watch Tyler's Adam's apple rising and falling as he swallows. The heat has made me thirsty and the cool of the can in my hand is tempting. I take a few steady sips. It's not so bad. The boys tip back their heads, drain their cans, give each other a nod then squash their empties and chuck them across the grass.

"Drink up," says Declan looking at me.

All three watch as I force down gulp after gulp. Maybe it's the heat, or the lack of food, but the alcohol goes straight to my head and it's taking the edge off my worry. I drink almost to the bottom then chuck my can to one side, as if it's something I do every day. The remaining contents seep out on to the grass.

There aren't many people about – a few dog-walkers and a woman out for a slow, effortful jog. I watch her with fascination, and giggle. Perhaps Liam and Tyler never went running at all – just came to the park and drank beer. The boys are in a bit of a huddle so I roll over onto my stomach and pick at blades of grass, building a small mound.

I see Tyler and Joel walking away. I jump to my feet too late. Declan puts his hand on my arm and holds me back.

"You're coming with me," he says.

I shake my head.

"Come on, live a little." He starts to walk and I find myself following. My feet are sluggish, my thoughts a little fuzzy.

We stop near the road in the shade of some trees. I can't see Tyler and Joel any more and I ask Declan where they've gone.

"Don't worry, they'll be back," he says. He's staring across the road and I lean slightly towards him to see what he is looking at.

"See over there?" Declan speaks quietly. "Number 27. I want you to go and ring on the doorbell."

"Why?"

"Because that's what I'm telling you to do."

Declan points at a smart house on the opposite side of the street. The door isn't clearly visible. The house is set back from the road by a gravelled, off-street parking area and separated from the pavement by a leafy ledge.

"If anyone answers," Declan continues, "Just say you're looking for Miranda Stackpoole."

I give a nervous laugh. "Who's she?"

Declan rolls his eyes. "Do you have to ask questions the whole time? It doesn't matter who she is."

"So I ask for Miranda Stackpoole and then. . . ?"

"Smile and be polite. They'll tell you she doesn't live there or something. You'll apologize and say you've made a mistake. You've been brought up nicely. I'm sure you can sound convincing."

"And if there's no answer?"

"Job done. You come back here and you wait."

I look at the door and then at the ground. Declan's feet are almost toe to toe with mine. I want to think this is some kind of game. My hands are clasped tightly together, so tight my knuckles are hurting.

"Is that it?" I say, looking up and forcing myself to meet his eyes. What I see makes me take a step back and then another. Each move I make, he follows. His eyes bore into me, a hint of amusement mixed with simmering menace and I'm like a trapped animal.

"OK," I say, because I know it is the only thing I can say.

Declan raises his eyebrows. I guess he was expecting me to refuse.

"Oh, and just so you are quite clear," he says, "you won't breathe a word of this to anybody. Ever. You're part of us now, Amber. You dob us in, we'll do worse to you."

The threat is clear and I understand this is not a game. Yet I sense a small opportunity.

"You promise to give me back my stone and I promise I'll keep quiet."

Declan laughs through his nose and shakes his head. I see his hand go to his pocket. I can't believe it's this easy. I hold out my hand for the stone.

In a moment I see a flash. No stone but the hard, shiny steel of a blade. For some reason, I try to laugh, but he's holding me close with one arm and pressing the knife against my shoulder with the other, the bone of his jaw jutting into the side of my head. Declan is threatening me with a knife.

"I don't negotiate," says Declan, keeping hold of me, "especially not with girls. You will do as you're told and you won't open your mouth. Do you understand? One word out of you and it won't just be you that gets it. It'll be your friend Tyler, too. And you wouldn't want that, would you? You've caused enough trouble already."

I'm trying to make sense of his words. I focus on the knife. All I can do is nod. He pushes me away roughly.

"Now go and knock on the door." He enunciates each word slow, through gritted teeth. I watch myself from a distance; I am someone else. "Miranda Stackpoole," I whisper.

"Good." He flips the knife back into his pocket. "Now get going and keep it natural." He unrolls a tote bag and hands it to me.

"What's this for?"

"Keep hold of it. There's a phone in there. See anything we should know about and you press the call button. Let it ring twice then cut off."

"Ring twice and cut off," I repeat like a puppet. I slip the handle of the bag over my shoulder.

He nods his head in the direction of the house and I take a couple of steps, but then he grabs the back of my shirt and pulls me back.

"Wait," he hisses down my ear. He holds me still

until the same slow jogger as before passes us –
she gives us a hard stare. We wait, rigid, until she's
panted her way down the street. Then he gives me a
push. I cross the road on to the pavement and make
my way over the gravel drive towards the door. I
try to look casual and relaxed. Miranda Stackpoole.
I say the name over and over. I pretend I'm doing
a dare like Liam and I used to do when we were
kids. We'd ring a doorbell then run away and hide –
except this time I mustn't run away or hide. This
time . . . I don't let myself think.

There's no sign of any car in the short driveway
in front of the door, but there's a light on inside.
I peer through the window, then ring the bell and
wait. There's no answer. I look back at Declan, but
I can hardly make him out in the shade of the trees.
I wait some more, kicking the step a few times
with the toe of my shoe. I ring one last time, more
confident now, leaving my finger on the bell. At least
I won't have to go through some stupid charade. By
the time I turn around again to check with Declan,
he's gone.

I do as I'm told and head back to the trees on the
edge of the park and sit down. I put my hand into
the bag, pull out the phone, examine it and put it

back. A car passes, but apart from that there's not much going on. I watch dark clouds slide across the sky. The atmosphere is heavy and close and my head has started to ache. I close my eyes then jump as a deep rumble of thunder grumbles across the distance.

The phone buzzes. Without thinking, I reach for the phone in the blue bag, but there's no message. Then I fumble in my pocket for my own. It's a text from Mum. She's on her way back from the hospital. Some sensible part of my brain tells me I need to get home. But I can't go home. I'm powerless and I'm scared. I hold my head.

"Come on," I say under my breath. "Come on, come on." I don't know if I'm talking to myself or to the others. I wait. The leaves on the trees rustle.

With a bang, the door of number 27 bursts open and I'm on my feet. Tyler's out of it, running fast, closely followed by Joel. There's muffled shouting from inside the house. Declan almost trips down the step, but gathers himself and keeps going. A woman is walking along the pavement pushing a baby in a buggy. Her face registers horror as Declan whacks straight into her, tipping the pushchair, spilling the child and the shopping on the ground. He doesn't stop. Instinctively, I move towards her to help, then my brain kicks in, everything moving in slow motion.

"Fucking run," yells Declan.

Another person races out of the house, a uniform. Sirens scream and reality kicks in hard. This is trouble and I'm part of it. Adrenaline throws my body into action and I start to sprint across the park after the others. I can hear the woman screaming abuse after us, the baby crying, more shouting and footsteps following me. I keep running, try to keep the others in sight, but they've split off in different directions. I clasp the bag to my chest, look over my shoulder, stumble, right myself, stumble again, my ankle going over. I can feel my fall in slow motion, hands going out, skidding away, chin hitting the grass, teeth against gum, scrabbling to get up but tripping again. Pressure on my shoulder and I'm caught.

I gulp for air, my cheek pressed to the ground, my hands pulled behind my back. I can taste the blood in my mouth, feel my world spinning out of control.

I hear words, some clear, some blurred. Something about *arrest* and *burglary* and *not trying to run.* I lie still, my whole body tense. The policeman seems to wait until he's certain that any resistance has gone out of me. He asks me my name. *Am I OK?* He helps me to my feet and I try for a nod, running my tongue along the inside of my lower lip and feeling the fullness of the rough, painful swelling. He has handcuffs in his hand, but he doesn't use them.

I search around for the others but there's no sign of them. I'm on my own.

They lead me towards the road, where there's a police car waiting. This can't be happening.

The policeman tells me to get in and a woman opens the door.

"No, wait. You don't understand. You have to listen to me; I haven't done anything."

"You can tell us all about it at the station," he says.

"Station – what station?"

He puts his hand on the top of my head and, automatically, I duck into the open door of the car.

"Amber. You did say your name was Amber, didn't you?" He leans into the back of the car as he speaks to me.

"Yes."

"You have been arrested. We're taking you to the police station. Do you understand?"

I process this along with the sounds and the smells and the feel of the seat against my legs.

I'm in a police car. I've been arrested. What do I do? What will my parents do? Oh God, what will they say? What will Gran think? This'll kill her. I have to stop them finding out. Declan never said – not in so many words. They could have been doing anything. How was I supposed to know? I shouldn't have run. If I hadn't run then the police might've thought I had nothing to do with it. I didn't have anything to do with it – not really.

Thoughts pile in, one on top of the other. Rewinding, replaying. Declan and Joel and Tyler in my kitchen. I should have stood up to them. I should've refused. Tears run down my cheeks, drip on to my jeans. I only rang a bloody doorbell. They can't send me to prison for ringing a doorbell, can they? It shouldn't be me in this car. It's not right. Why did I bloody run? I'm an idiot, a stupid, stupid idiot.

The car starts to move and I stare out of the window, watching the streets go by, strange and unreal. Do I look like a criminal? My throat constricts making breathing hard as frustration hammers against my ribs at the injustice of it all.

It's Tyler's fault. I want to kill him. How did he pull me in so easily? All his promises, his lines about needing me, about my brother wanting us to be together. Did he have this planned all along? Is this what he did to my brother? I bet he never gave a toss about Liam, just like he doesn't give a toss about me. If he did, he'd have come back for me. He's only loyal to one person. Declan.

And what are they all doing now, as I'm being driven to the police station? Lounging around in the caravan, no doubt, drinking the rest of the beer, smoking, laughing at me, laughing at their lucky escape. Becky will be there, flashing her tits at Declan. He's probably given her Liam's stone to wear. Anger flares, and the need for revenge. I could tell the police where they are. I could take them straight there. For a moment I feel light-headed with the idea until Declan's threats come thundering in; the knife held against me. My thoughts turn on their head. What if I'm wrong and Tyler does care about me and he's as scared and hurt and confused as I am? I'm in this as deep as I can get and I can't risk saying anything, because I don't trust anyone any more. I hate Declan, I hated him from the start, and now I'm very, very afraid.

I give one small sob, digging the nails of one hand into the back of the other in an effort at control. The policeman looks at me as if he's seen it all before. He *has* seen it all before. I'm just another bad kid like so many others round here. Why would he think I'm any different?

At that moment the rain starts. Slow at first then pounding against the windscreen, the wipers frantically flipping back and forth, back and forth. It makes me cold and it makes me sad.

I wish I was Liam. I wish I was dead.

CHAPTER 16

The police station is a modern building with a lot of glass. You can see out of the windows but you can't see in. That makes me feel better. I don't want anyone to see me. But there are eyes everywhere and I can't hide.

I'm taken to the custody suite where a policeman stands at a desk behind a glass screen and reads me my rights. I nod as I try to take in what he's saying, but his words disappear into a fog of fear. He asks me my name and address and tells me they need to inform my parents. I wish I could disappear for ever. The thought of what Dad is going to say is almost worse than being arrested.

In another room a lady in a uniform searches me and takes my watch, my jewellery and the laces out of my shoes. They already have my phone and the small amount of money I had in my pockets. They've got the bag Declan gave me too. Then I'm asked some questions by someone who I think is a nurse or a doctor. Have I drunk any alcohol, taken any substances? Yes to the alcohol – not much. I answer all her questions and she seems satisfied. I'm offered water. Do I need the toilet? I shake my head to both.

Then I'm led through a heavy door and straight ahead, across a corridor, into a white-walled room with a wooden bench and a hard floor. This, I'm informed, is a detention room. It looks like a cell to me – a cell for criminals – and it's so bare it makes me feel naked.

"We'll let you know when your dad arrives," says the policewoman. And the door is closed. It feels final, as if I'll be locked in for ever. I know it's not cold, but I'm shivering and I curl up into a ball in the corner. In a room like this you can't look outwards, only inwards. And I don't want to look inwards because every thought is a bad thought. There's nowhere I can go in my head that doesn't fill me with panic or fear. There's a kind of peephole in the door so that people on the outside can watch without me knowing. I picture Liam watching me. *Finders keepers, losers weepers.*

I don't know how long I wait. I rehearse what I'm going to say to Dad. I go over and over what happened. Every small sound is magnified. With each click or bang, I expect the door to open and Dad to come in. I wonder if any of the others are in here. For all I know, Tyler could be next door, but something tells me he isn't.

By the time the door does open, I've almost given up. Suddenly Dad is here in the room and I don't know what to do. I want him to hold out his arms and tell me everything will be all right, but he stands stiffly, creating an invisible wall between us.

"What the hell have you done?" he asks. He stares around and shakes his head. "God!"

I stand up, but he holds up his hand in a "stop" motion. Tears threaten and I try to swallow and blink them back. Dad seems uncertain as to what happens next and an officer reads my rights again and asks me and Dad if we understand. Dad nods.

"Right, Mr Neville, your daughter will be held here pending enquiries. You will be required to be present at the interview. Do you wish to contact a solicitor or we can contact a solicitor on your behalf?"

Dad shakes his head. I don't know if he's taking in anything at all.

"There may be a considerable delay before the interview. You can either wait in the waiting room or go home and we'll contact you."

Dad shakes his head again.

"How long?" I ask. I don't want to be in this room any longer.

"Depends on how long it takes," says the officer.

Dad doesn't even look at me before he leaves. He's only been here a matter of minutes. The door bangs shut and I'm alone again. Time becomes my central focus, but without a watch I have no idea of how many hours pass. I count to sixty a few times, trying to measure the length of a minute. I need to keep my mind busy to stop fear taking over. I don't want to think about what's happened. I've already been over it in my head a hundred times. I'm exhausted and wide awake at the same time. I'm offered food and more water, but I can't touch anything.

Finally, I hear the click of the door and I'm on my feet before it's open. I'm taken to an interview room. Dad is waiting, big and bristling and we sit down opposite two more police officers. The interview is horrendous. Question after question after question. It gets worse and worse. I tell them exactly what happened. I don't bother to lie. They keep delving deeper and deeper until I know I'm bad from head to toe.

They ask me why I have two phones and I tell them I only have one. They ask about the other one, the one in the bag.

"Nothing to do with me," I say. This doesn't feel like too much of a lie.

"So how come it was in your bag, Amber?"

"It isn't my bag."

"Oh, for goodness' sake," says Dad.

"I mean I was given it by . . . by one of the others." I pull myself up quickly just before I say Declan's name. "The phone was in it. I was supposed to use it to ring if I saw anything."

"Anything. . . ?"

I shrug. "I didn't use it."

The police officer makes a note.

They ask me about my own phone and who I've contacted recently. It occurs to me then that none of the group ever contacted me by phone. I never had any of their mobile numbers either. No trace at all. Was that on purpose? Were they that clever?

I don't have time to think too hard about this. The questions keep coming.

I have to go over my movements over the last few days and that's trickier. I talk about working at the café and they ask me about Cathy, Simon and the new boy, Josh.

"Surely you're not suggesting Cathy or Simon are involved in all this?" Dad says. He sounds ready to explode.

"We're not suggesting anything," the policeman says.

They ask Dad if he can vouch for my movements and he says he can. I can feel my eyes widening in disbelief, but I force myself to nod in agreement. He tells them I've been grounded since Kelly's party and that's why he's so shocked about what's happened. Dad makes himself sound like the super-responsible parent, but I'm not sure they buy it.

Then they ask me about Kelly's party. How do I know her? Who was there? Who did I talk to? I tell them the truth – that I didn't really know anyone. They get impatient. So does Dad.

"We told you to stay away from that girl," he says.

"Was Kelly involved?" they ask me.

"No," I answer truthfully.

Dad huffs, sits back in his chair and folds his arms.

Repeatedly, they ask me to name the other members of the gang. And I want to. I want to spill them all out, tell them everything. I scream at myself, *tell them, tell them*, but Declan's voice screams back louder. I need time to think this through, but time is something I don't have. If Declan's threats are real . . . *give us names, Amber* . . . and they are real . . . *give us names* . . . what will he do to me? What will he do to Tyler? *NAMES*.

I shake my head. If I say anything, anything at all, Declan will know. I don't want Declan coming after me. I have to protect myself. And I don't want Tyler getting hurt. I have to protect him too — even after what he's done — because I don't know anything for sure. Tyler said we must stick together, for Liam's sake, but what's Liam got to do with all this? Nothing makes sense any more. Every nerve in my body is ragged and raw.

"I can't tell you?" I whisper.

"Can't or won't?" says Dad. "Just bloody tell them the names."

I look at Dad and I wish he would understand I

don't need more enemies. A long silence follows. A silence I am expected to fill. If Dad had been the perfect father he's making himself out to be, he never would have left me on the anniversary of Liam's death and none of this would've happened. Or I would've told him about Declan after that day in the shopping mall and perhaps he would have helped. Who knows? But I've never really talked to Dad – not ever. I had Liam.

The silence continues.

I press my lips together and give a small shrug. I sense, in the eyes of the people questioning me, that they understand more than Dad. I want them to know that I am not being difficult for the sake of it. I want them to see the battle going on in my head.

The interview winds up. Every last bit of energy, every morsel of information has been sucked from me. Everything except names or any other specifics about Tyler, Declan, Joel or Becky.

The policeman says that I'll be released on bail pending further enquiries. I don't know what this means but I cling on to the word *released*.

"Does that mean I can go home?" I ask.

"Yes."

"Now?"

"Yes. You will be required to return to this station in one month's time unless you are contacted before that date."

"Will I go to prison?"

At the mention of the word prison, Dad runs his fingers through his hair and slumps back in his chair.

"All the information will be passed to the Youth Offending Team and you'll be contacted by them in due course."

Before I leave, I'm fingerprinted and photographed, my personal identity recorded for ever, and my things returned to me – all except my phone. Getting out of here is the only thing I care about and, as we walk towards the door, my legs almost give way with relief. It doesn't last long. I feel Dad's grip on my arm, I feel Declan's knife pressing against me, Liam's shadow, my guilt. I've been released but I'm not free.

It's almost dark when we step out of the station and on to the wet pavement. After the silence of my cell and the noiselessness of the interview room, the sound of traffic, the sloosh of tyres on the slick wet road surface, feels like an attack. The streets have changed. There's no comfortable familiarity any more. I don't know who, or what, or where to trust. I feel watched.

Dad has his arm linked through mine, pinning my elbow to his side. I'd like to know what's going on in his head. We walk together, Dad with his head down, me trying to see behind every car, around every corner. I try to comfort myself with the fact I'm going home and, right now, home seems like a good option. But is it a safe option? Of course it isn't. They know where I live.

Dad unlocks the car and we get in, still without saying a word. I slide my hand to the manual lock button near the handle and press, listening for the gentle click that tells me my door can't be opened from the outside. Then we sit. Dad makes no move to drive away. We sit and sit until I can't stand it any longer.

"I'm sorry," I mumble.

He takes a deep breath and throws back his head, hitting the steering wheel with the palms of his hands. It scares me and I shrink back towards my door, trying to disappear into my seat.

When he looks at me his eyes are raging, but when he speaks his anger is matter-of-fact and controlled.

"We'll never forgive you for this, Amber. Don't expect anything from your mother and me any more. Nothing. Do you understand?"

I nod wearily. I don't expect much as it is. Are they going to throw me out? Take away my job? Or is it just another empty threat?

Dad starts the car, reverses out of the parking space too fast, and drives us home. My mind is numb and exhausted. When we arrive, I trail behind him into the house.

"Paula?" shouts Dad as he shuts the door. There's no answer. He goes upstairs and when he comes down, his eyes tell me all I need to know about the state Mum's in. I don't know how to act or what I'm supposed to do, so I put on the kettle. Dad's mobile rings and he goes off into another room. I make us both tea. It feels normal, but it isn't.

He looks hassled when he comes back into the kitchen and when I push a cup of tea towards him, he takes it without a word of thanks.

"I'm off tomorrow, early," he says. "I won't be back for a few days. If you do anything, ANYTHING to cause trouble, you'll be out of this house for good. Do you understand?"

I take in what he is saying, but the words don't carry any weight. I've heard it all before.

"Turn out the lights before you go to bed," he says and I count his treads up the stairs. Eleven, twelve, thirteen.

Bed. It's where I need to be. I stand up and glimpse a movement at the kitchen window. I freeze, my heart pounding. The movement freezes with me and I realize it's my own reflection, shadowy and scary. I check all the windows are tight closed and pull down the blinds, shutting out the dark. I don't want to think of the last time I was in this kitchen. I don't want to think of Declan. I let the numbness come over me again and I fear going to sleep and losing control. So I sit down in the quiet, put my cheek down on the table, and stare at the wall.

CHAPTER 17

I have no idea when I eventually crawl into bed. My body is desperate for sleep but my mind is still working overtime. I turn on the light, turn it off again. I lie on my side, my back, my stomach. Finally I hug my duvet around me and watch the dawn light creep through the curtains. I keep thinking, over and over, that all this is some big mistake; that I wasn't actually there; that it wasn't me that got arrested. It doesn't feel like me. It doesn't even look like me. This is a person I don't know.

Dad is quiet as he gets up and it's not long before I hear his car start and pull away. I'm glad I don't have to see him. I'm glad he's gone. I don't care if I never see him again. I don't care if I never see anyone again. I give sleep one last try but it's useless; my heart is beating too hard, my panic uncontainable.

I have to move, so I stand up and peep through the curtains. The world is still there. It hasn't ended. I check up and down the street. It looks the same as usual. Normality still exists for those who are lucky.

I tug the curtains open and sit back down on the bed. I look at the books school has given me to read over the holidays. I was hoping to carry on with English next year, but now I'm not even sure that school will have me back. Will they know? Will everyone know? I can imagine them talking about me in huddled groups. Or maybe not. Maybe people getting in trouble with the police is so common at school that no one will notice. *But AMBER*, I can hear them saying in a tone somewhere between shock and excitement. First my brother, now this. Why?

The empty space where I used to hide Liam's stone glares at me. My mind travels up endless dead ends. Each time, I feel another speck of hope crushed out of me. My gut spasms and I have to run to the toilet.

By nine o'clock the sun is bright. I lie, curled even tighter on my bed, holding my belly. It's more habit than anything that sends me through to Mum's room. I want to tell her my tummy hurts and I want to crawl into bed with her and for her to bring a towel and bowl "just in case". But when I tiptoe into her room, smell the fug and see the way her arm hangs over the edge of the bed, I know it's me that should be fetching the towel and bowl.

I can't do this by myself. I can't.

I walk slowly down the stairs, feeling each step. Simon? I take a deep breath. I know I can't ring Simon. Other friends? Where have all my friends gone? I wander into the kitchen. I'd like to open a window, but I don't dare.

Stuck to the fridge is a list of hospital information. I run my finger down the list of numbers. Ward G5 has been added to the bottom. That must be where Gran is now. My finger hovers over the number. I memorize it.

I pick up the phone then put it down again. Why ring? If I ring she can refuse to see me. If I go to the hospital, it'll be much harder for her to turn me away. It may not work but it's the best chance I've got. G5.

I choose my clothes carefully. It matters that I look nice on the outside and concentrating on the little things helps. The journey to the hospital takes for ever. I feel as if everyone's eyes are on me; as if they all know. In turn, I'm watchful. It's tiring. The doors hiss open and shut. The bus gets more and more crowded and stepping off brings a brief sense of escape.

Walking through the entrance of the hospital is like walking into a part of my mind that I prefer to keep closed. Bit by bit, the wall I have built so carefully is crumbling. I try to blank out arriving here with PC Marsh, taking the lift to intensive care, seeing Tyler's face. Too late. I was too late.

I need flowers. There's nothing very pretty except for roses, which are too expensive. I settle for a bunch of something without too much orange. Gran doesn't like orange flowers. I follow the signs to the ward and rehearse what I'm going to say.

The ward is divided into a number of rooms, each with six beds. I peer through trying to spot Gran, but a lot of the beds have curtains drawn around them.

A nurse stops me. "I'm afraid it's not visiting hours," she says. "You'll have to come back at three. Who have you come to see?"

"My gran. Mrs Turner."

I stand clasping my bunch of flowers. I hadn't even thought about visiting times. It's only just after 11a.m. and I can hardly sit and wait for four hours.

Tears of frustration fill my eyes. "Please," I say. The nurse seems to calculate the situation and tells me to wait a moment.

When she comes back, she's smiling and her voice has softened. "Your gran is with the physio at the moment but they're nearly through. You can pop in after that. Not for long, though – and don't tell anyone! Take a seat in here and I'll come and get you when she's ready." She shows me into a room with chairs and a fish tank.

"Thank you," I say and I mean it with every bit of my being. "Don't tell her I'm here," I say. "I want it to be a surprise."

"All right," she says, and hands me a box of tissues from the side. "Your gran is doing well. She should be home by the end of the week. Cheer up – she's going to be OK."

I wipe away the remainder of my tears.

So much has happened since I last saw Gran. She's been cocooned here in hospital while my life spirals out of control.

A frail old woman comes in, taking unsteady steps behind her walking frame. She's concentrating hard. A nurse is with her, hands out either side, ready to catch. The old lady stops when she gets to me and admires the flowers. She's spilt something down the front of her dressing gown. "Learning to walk again," she says, grinning, as she staggers forward. The nurse dances around behind her. Encouraging.

"You're doing well," I say. I can't imagine what it must be like to lose the ability to walk.

Can Gran walk? I hadn't thought about that. How will she look? I don't want Gran to have spills down her dressing gown. She's fussy about the way she looks. I wait and wait until I wonder if the nurse has forgotten about me. The old lady comes round for a second time and her movements seem less effortful.

"You'll be on the running track soon," I say and she loves that.

I flick through a magazine without focusing on anything and finally the nurse comes back and I follow her along the corridor. Gran is in a room at the far corner of the ward, and she's sitting on a chair between her bed and the window. She does look thinner and very tired, but her hair is brushed. A man in a white top and blue trousers is busy organizing a pile of cushions around her and Gran doesn't notice me at first. Seeing her, sitting up and alive, makes me want to burst with happiness.

I move forward slowly, glancing at the rows of get well cards for my own. It's behind the jug of orange squash, so at least Mum gave it to her. Gran is still fussing around, trying to get comfortable, and then she sees me.

"Hello!" There's question, surprise, but not a hint of anger in her voice. "This is my granddaughter," she says to the physio. "Amber."

"Hi," he says, smiling. "I'll leave you to it then. See you tomorrow, Mrs Turner. Don't forget to do your feet exercises. Three times a day – more if you can."

My own feet seem stuck to the floor.

"Well," says Gran. "It's you. I was wondering when you were going to come and see me."

"I wanted to come before but. . ."

"Don't just stand there," she says, her face breaking into a huge smile. "Come and give me a hug."

I try to hide my confusion and try to smile back. The upright chair and cushions and flowers make hugging awkward and it's more of a lean than a hug. She pats my shoulder. It all feels wrong. She doesn't smell like Gran, she smells like hospital, and it's a smell I associate with death.

"I've brought you these," I say and hold out my flowers. "Sorry, they're not very exciting."

She takes them and sniffs them. "Mmmm," she says, "they're lovely. We can throw out those old ones and put yours here in instead. You could do that for me if you like. Look, there's a bin in the corner over there."

I do as she says and it gives me a little time to pull myself together. When I've finished, I perch on the edge of her bed. It's hard and uncomfortable and it makes a strange noise every time I move.

"You were lucky they let you in," she says. "They're quite strict about visiting times."

"I'm sorry. I know you didn't want to see me." I hang my head.

"Who said I didn't want to see you?" Gran sounds very put out. I wonder if her memory has gone or something.

"I don't blame you," I say, "I know this was all my fault"

Gran is frowning now. "Amber, who told you that I didn't want to see you?"

"Dad. . . Mum." I stare down at my feet.

"Is that what they said?" She pauses. "Look at me. Did they tell you I didn't want to see you?"

I nod, miserably and then I give a small shrug.

"What I said was that I didn't want you to see me like *this*," she sweeps her hand across her body. "I didn't want you coming to the hospital and getting all upset. I certainly didn't want you to see me when I was half dead because no one wants to be seen when they're blue about the edges. But I never said that I didn't want to see you."

I try to remember Dad's exact words.

"I thought you were so angry at me."

"Why would you think that?"

"Because of what happened. Because I made you have a heart attack."

"Well, you may be a clever girl, but I can assure you that even you couldn't make me have a heart attack."

"But the party!"

Gran waves her hand in the air as if wafting away a bad smell. "Oh, well that, yes, it was a bit stressful and it probably didn't help. But I knew you'd be all right. This old heart of mine had been jangling warning bells for a while. It was going to happen some time."

But it didn't happen some time. It happened when I didn't turn up to meet her. The same as Liam happened – or stopped happening – after I took his stone. The same as Granddad when I smoked in his shed.

Gran crosses her arms and gives me her not-serious cross look. "I hope you're not going to sit there looking miserable. I need cheering up. So do you by the looks of things."

All I can think about is explaining to Gran what happened.

"My phone was stolen," I say. "And all my money – at the party, I mean. That's why I couldn't call you. And the party was awful so I left and spent the night with a friend. But we overslept and. . ."

Gran continues to wave the information away. "Let's forget all that. No good crying over spilt milk. I'll be out of here by the end of the week and I don't want you to think any more about it. Everything is fine."

The problem is, everything is not fine and that's what I need to talk to her about.

"Tell me what you've been up to while I've been lying around in here," she says, her voice full of enthusiastic encouragement. "Has the café been busy?"

I press my hand into a fist in front of my mouth; holding in the words. How can I begin to tell her? I can't. It'll make her ill again.

"Amber?" she says. "Are you all right?"

I nod. I shouldn't have come.

Her smile goes. "Is it Mum? Dad?" She leans forward slightly in her chair.

I drop my hand, but clamp my teeth over my bottom lip. I don't know where to start – or if to start. The words I'd rehearsed have gone.

"I can't help unless you talk to me," she says gently.

My fist hammers up and down on my leg, faster and faster. Gran puts her hand over it. "Take a breath," she says.

I take three. "I got arrested. Yesterday."

Gran goes very still. It's the only outward sign she gives of surprise.

"Are you going to tell me what for?" Her voice is calm and measured. I can only imagine what's going on inside.

"Burglary – or helping with a burglary – I mean I didn't actually steal anything myself – I didn't even go into the house."

Gran blinks a lot, as if trying to take in what I'm

telling her. "But you were there and you knew." She nods as she speaks.

"Yes, I was there. Yes, I suppose I knew. I'd had a bit to drink. They made me ring the doorbell. That's all I did. Ring the bell. Then I think I was supposed to keep watch and . . . I don't know what happened after that. They were ages and then the police came and I tripped and fell when I was trying to run away . . . I was the only one that got caught." The unfairness of it rips through me again.

"Slow down, slow down," says Gran. "They. You said *they* made you ring the doorbell. Who are *they*?"

I drop my eyes and press my lips together.

"I see," she says. "And did you tell the police who they were?"

"No. I can't. If I do. . ." I shift my position on the bed and it squishes uncomfortably. ". . . I don't know what will happen if I do – bad things."

Gran turns and looks out of the window. She twists her wedding ring round and round – the wedding ring she can't get over her knuckle any more. "Threats are a sign of weakness, you know." She turns back to me. "Mostly it's words – but you'll have to be the judge of that. I can understand you're frightened but you need to think about it very carefully."

How does Gran know? Has someone talked to her? A mesh of unspoken thoughts hovers in the air between us and her eyes travel over me, making me self-conscious.

"What happens next?" she asks.

"I don't know." My shoulders slump. "I'll hear from the police within the month. The youth someone or other. Then I have to go back to the police station. I don't know what will happen to me." I grip the blanket on the bed and try to stay calm.

"It's good you're scared," she says. "You should be. You've made a bad mistake."

"I've made lots of bad mistakes. It was a mistake I was born." I snap it out. It's anger at myself, not Gran.

"Sshhh," she says. "We all make plenty of bad mistakes. I could write a book about mine." She laughs, then becomes serious again. "I can't pretend that I'm not upset and disappointed, of course I am, but I have a feeling this situation isn't entirely of your own making. I'm not just talking about these others who were with you. I'm talking about me and your mum and dad. One thing I know for sure, you're not a bad girl, not really. I don't want you to think I'm making excuses for you, because I'm not, but sometimes it's hard to be perfect in an imperfect world."

I cover my eyes with my hands and shake my head.

"I do understand," she continues.

Old people always think they understand. The problem is, they don't, so whatever they say isn't quite right.

"I'm going to tell you a little secret," she says.

Here we go, I think. A moral tale, no doubt. She waits until I look at her.

"I was in trouble once. A long time ago." Her gaze shifts back to outside the window. "I got involved with the wrong people – bad people. They were using fraud to get money from the company we worked for. I was just an office junior. But I was easily influenced and I thought I was in love. And then it all fell apart and when I threatened to expose them, they blackmailed me. I know what it's like to feel threatened. In my case, it was so bad, I had to get away. That's how I ended up in France. I know what's happening to you is different and I know a lot of things have changed since I was young. But when I say I understand, I mean it."

It takes time to process what Gran is telling me. I'd heard rumours, but I'd never imagined that it was anything serious.

"Mum never told me."

"That's because your mum doesn't know. No one does. Except your granddad – and now you. My secret is safe with him and I trust it'll be safe with you too. It's not something I'm proud of."

"I won't tell anyone," I say. "Cross my heart and hope to die."

She smiles. "I'd rather you didn't hope to die. You've got a big life ahead of you."

I try to think about what might be asked, but only bad things come to mind.

"I wish I could go to France."

She squeezes my hand in hers and turns it over as if reading my palm. "One day maybe you can. But it's not the answer. You can't run away from guilt and responsibility."

I know I won't be able to stop the tears. I try to choke them back but they escape. What did I think? That Gran could wave a magic wand and make everything go away?

Gran pulls me towards her. I kneel on the floor and rest my head on her lap. For a few minutes, sandwiched between a bed and a window in the corner of a hospital ward, I feel totally safe with the only person in the world who still cares about me. She strokes my hair gently.

"You see, you need to find a way to make peace with yourself. It's not good enough to be sorry – you have to do something to prove it to yourself and to others. That's the only way to move forward."

My tears drop on to Gran's dressing gown. I feel them trickling over the bridge of my nose and across my cheek.

"But what can I do?"

"You'll find a way. Or, most likely, a way will find you. That's what usually happens."

"Not in my case."

"We'll see," she says soothingly. "We'll see." Her hand makes small circles on my back.

I hope she's right, but the trouble is she only knows the half of it. How can I make peace with myself when I'm so angry, so resentful, so confused? How can I do anything when Declan, Joel and Tyler are still out there? There's too much stuff that's

234

unresolved. I want to be safe; I want to be normal again.

"Do you ever think about Liam?" I ask Gran.

"Of course I do."

"Do you think we could've saved him, if we'd known in time?" I say. "Or do you believe in fate?"

At once she goes very still and I look up to make sure she's OK. She's frowning. She doesn't speak for a while. I want her to give me an answer.

"That's a big question and one I'm sure we've all asked ourselves a thousand times. And I don't know. Liam might have survived if it had been diagnosed. He would have had a lifetime of drugs and there would have been limits on what he was allowed to do. Ultimately, he might have needed a new heart. On the other hand, it may have made no difference."

"Do you think other things could have played a part – like stress maybe – or fear?"

"Of course things like that can make a difference. He pushed his body to the limit. It was amazing there weren't more warning signs. But he certainly never struck me as very stressed. And what did he have to fear?"

I give the smallest shrug.

"You have to let Liam go. We all take secrets to the grave. I agree that it feels like a mistake in the master plan when a young person dies — but ours is not to reason why. If your time is up, your time is up."

"And you believe that?"

"Yes, Amber. I do."

CHAPTER 18

I leave the hospital and turn my face to the sun. I hold on to everything Gran said. I use it as my crutch to get through each day.

I'm expected to carry on life as normal: to go to work, come home, be the same. How can I be the same? I'm not the same. The one thing Gran can't do is take away the threats or the uncertainty. I don't know what's going to happen to me, what the police are going to do with me. I don't trust days any more – or times, or places, or people. Don't get me wrong. I'm not expecting sympathy, but nothing in my life could have prepared me for this and I don't know how to deal with it.

Dad told me we could keep it all quiet, but news travels fast and everyone likes a bit of gossip. First Liam, now me. We've given the neighbours plenty to talk about. It's easier to avoid seeing people I know so I keep my head down and try not to be noticed. Oddly enough, working at the café isn't too bad. There are a few regulars – but no one who knows me well.

Simon's mum has been on the phone to Dad, ranting on about me giving Simon's name to the police and getting him into trouble. Apparently, I'm to stay away from Simon. Evidently Simon doesn't talk to his mum or she'd know we're not seeing each other anyway.

So when the café door opens on Friday morning, and Simon walks in, I'm more than surprised.

"Hi," he says, casual as anything. "I was hoping you'd be here."

I feel like we're strangers. I don't know what to say to him. Simon who I know so well.

"Can I get you something?" I ask.

"Water would be good. I'll get it."

There are jugs on the side nearby and he pours himself a large glass and gulps it down.

"Your mum says I have to stay away from you. Did you know that?" I try to make a joke of it.

Simon laughs drily. "Yep. Mum's reputation has been damaged *for ever* since the police turned up at our door. She doesn't seem so worried about my reputation."

"I'm sorry. I didn't mean to get you into trouble. I never said anything bad about you."

He pulls out a chair and sits down. "I think they were following up on your phone contacts. You had messages on your phone from me. Nothing I couldn't explain."

I pull my shoulders right up to my ears and then drop them again. I don't know what I can say.

"Forget it," he says. "It wasn't that much of a big deal and it's not why I've come."

"Oh." I rub my hands up and down my legs. I can't bring myself to meet his eyes.

He leans back and taps the table. "Do you think Cathy would mind if we have a quick talk. It's important."

The café is empty apart from one other customer. I go out to the kitchen and Cathy looks surprised when I tell her Simon is here. "Fine," she says. "We're hardly busy." I return to the table, sit down opposite him and wait out an awkward silence.

"So," he says. "How are you?"

"Yeah — good." He looks at me unblinking — sceptical. I take a deep breath. "OK, well the last few weeks haven't exactly been the best of my life."

"And your gran?"

"Home. Mum's looking after her."

Simon widens his eyes in amazement. "She's home already? That's incredible. And your mum is looking after her?"

"I know. Sounds unlikely, but Mum's been pretty good lately. Looking after Gran has given her a sense of purpose. She's only been on a couple of benders, which isn't that surprising given what's been going on."

Simon shrugs. "So who's looking after you?"

"Dad's home a bit." I leave it at that. Dad's made it quite clear that it's a massive inconvenience having to stick around so that he can *keep an eye on* me. His version of keeping an eye on me seems to involve seeing as little of me as possible. He locks himself away with his phone and the computer and has murmured conversations for hours and hours. He must use up all his talk because he's got none left for anyone else. As long as I can account for my every move, that's where his interest starts and stops.

"What about you?" I ask. This stilted conversation with Simon is embarrassing and ridiculous.

"I've started working at the gym round the

corner from home. I'm mainly on reception at the moment, but they're giving me training and I get free membership. I've been working out a bit."

"Sounds good."

"I had to find some way to sort myself out." He drops his eyes and I know it's a dig at me but I'm not going to rise to the bait.

"You should try some of my life," I tell you.

He picks up a fork from the table and turns it over in his hands. "That's kind of why I'm here. I've been worried about you."

"Thanks."

"No, I mean it, and I should've got in contact before."

"Simon, you said you needed some time apart from me. I get that. It's fine. Leave it. I don't want to cause you any more trouble." I pretend to be cool about this, but I realize how much I've missed Simon; how nice it is to have him sitting here with me.

"No, it's not fine. I think I could have warned you before all this happened." He grinds the end of the fork into the table.

"What are you talking about?"

Another awkward silence — as if he's in two minds whether to carry on or not.

"Maybe it's nothing." He's lowered his voice, leaning forward so our heads are close together. He's put the fork down and he's pressing down on the prongs, making the other end bounce up and down on the table. It's distracting. "The police come round to my place on the day after you were arrested and they ask me a million questions about how I know you, where I was on the day of the burglary, could anyone vouch for me. That kind of thing. It wasn't hard to answer their questions and they didn't have a problem with any of it except. . ."

"Except what?"

"Except they seemed particularly interested in Kelly."

"Yeah, they asked me a lot about Kelly too." I shift in my chair, trying to work out where this is leading. "So what did you tell them?"

"Her dad's in prison, you know."

I lean back in my chair. "He's always in prison. It's hardly a state secret."

Simon shrugs. "I told them I knew Kelly a little. They asked me about the night of her party – all those messages on your phone. They wanted to know if I knew where you were."

My heart beats faster. "Did you tell them?"

"Yeah. I said you were with Kelly's brother."

"You told them I was with Tyler?"

"Well, you were, weren't you?"

I close my eyes and try to calm myself. I can't believe the police haven't called me back in. If Simon's given them Tyler's name then I'm dead. Or he is.

Simon touches my hand. "If Tyler's got you wrapped up in all this, then you need to tell the police."

"There's no need to get carried away." I try to keep the worry out of my voice, but Simon knows a lot more than I'm comfortable with.

"Kelly's been telling me one or two things about her brother."

"*Step*brother — and since when have you been having heart-to-hearts with Kelly?"

Simon doesn't say anything. I swear to God he's blushing.

"I . . . we've met up. A couple of times."

"Oh yeah?"

He shifts himself away from me. "It was you who invited me along to her party." I recognize the resentment simmering below the surface. "You sent me God knows how many texts. I turn up.

You're nowhere to be found. No answer from your phone. How do you think I felt?" He sighs loudly. "I decided I may as well have a good time. I got pissed – probably worse. Ended up with Kelly – DON'T say anything. Mistake – maybe. But she's OK. You used to be friends once, remember? She actually cares about you. And yes, we've met up a couple of times since."

I can't believe what I'm hearing. "So why did you give me all that rubbish about leaving the café because of me? Why didn't you just tell me you were seeing Kelly?" I try to ignore twinges of jealousy – twinges I've got no right to feel.

"Because I'm not seeing Kelly – or not like that. Look, forget about me and Kelly." He lowers his voice again. "Did you know that it was Tyler who got Kelly to invite you to the party? Which was odd since she said Tyler wasn't invited himself. . ."

"Half the people there weren't invited."

His eyes search mine. "She told me he kept on and on at her – said it was the right thing to do as you'd be feeling sad and all that. She agreed and then, out of the blue, Tyler turns up and whisks you away. She thinks he set you up on purpose."

"That's rubbish. The only reason I bumped into

him was because my bag was stolen. I was about to leave."

Simon picks up the fork again. "Apparently he lives in a caravan somewhere out of town. Kelly says he hangs out with a bunch of weirdos."

"I wouldn't know who he hangs out with."

"She says she knows how these people operate. She says if you get sucked in you're sunk."

I fold my arms and try to look relaxed. "Kelly's full of crap."

"Is she, though? Why would she make it up?"

"You know how she likes to overdramatize things."

"No, I don't." He stretches his arms and pushes away from the table. "So you're telling me all this – this burglary and your arrest and everything – has got nothing to do with Tyler?"

I shake my head, my energy slipping away. Lying does that to you. It drains you. But the last thing I want is for Simon to get involved. I don't want him being dragged into this mess.

"You've never been a good liar," he says. "I know you too well. You need to tell the police. If you don't, I will." He throws down the challenge as if it's some kind of game.

I tip my head back and close my eyes. When I open them again, Simon is watching me. "You don't know anything," I say.

"Why are you trying to protect him?"

I look away again, rub the top of my arm with my hand.

"You admit it then — you are trying to protect him. I thought you said nothing was going on between you two?"

It's not fair, Simon doing this to me. He wouldn't if he knew.

"I'll tell you what's going on between us. He's the only person who's ever talked to me about my brother since he died. He made me feel normal, for once, or at least that I'm not the only one struggling to cope. He knows how it feels to be in my situation. He was Liam's best friend."

"So you keep saying. But that only makes it easier for him to manipulate you. What do you know about him really? You used to complain that Liam changed when he was around Tyler. You'd come into the café grumbling about it. I got the impression you didn't like him much. Now, suddenly, he's your new best friend and you're the one who's changed. Seems a bit of a coincidence."

"Tyler is not a bad guy. You need to leave this alone."

Simon holds up his hands. "I don't know what's going on and if you don't want to tell me then that's up to you. All I'm saying is I think it's possible Tyler is using you. You need to take care."

I recognize what he's telling me. It's not as if I haven't thought it myself in my blackest moments. But some part of me refuses to believe Tyler is all bad. I cover my face with my hands and try to think. When I lean forward and clasp my hands together on the table, Simon does the same. It's disconcerting.

"I know you're trying to help," I say, "but I need you to promise me you won't go to the police and start making accusations. If you do, then I could end up in a lot more trouble than I'm in now. If you really care about me then you'll keep quiet. Just for the time being – for your own sake and mine. Please."

We hold each other's gaze, his eyes searching for information that I'm not going to give him.

"OK. But if I promise not to do anything, you have to promise not to go anywhere near Tyler Dawson."

"Don't worry. I won't be seeing him."

"Promise?"

I nod.

"You can call me," he says. "If anything happens or you need me – call – OK?"

I smile at him. "No phone," I say, spreading my hands.

He's so bloody nice and I have no idea why he bothers with me at all. If anything happened to Simon, I would never forgive myself. So, right now, all I need is for Simon to keep quiet. He knows enough to be dangerous and it's bad enough the police know I was with Tyler after Kelly's party. I've been kidding myself I can get through this – but now I'm not so sure.

CHAPTER 19

The full impact of everything Simon said seeps slowly into my bones, increasing my fear and messing with my head a little more. I don't know if the police have done anything with the information that Simon's given them, but suddenly Declan's threats seem much closer.

In fact everything seems much closer because the Youth Offending Team is on to my case and I have now been assigned a caseworker. She's coming to visit me for the first time this morning. Her name is Siân. She'll be coming to my house at 10.30 and I watch the clock tick away the time. Dad was supposed to be here but he's been called away on urgent business. He and Mum argued last night, the walls of our house not thick enough for me to hide from the details. *How can you leave me to deal with this? Is she more important?* I could only suppose *this* was me. I didn't want to think about the rest so I shut myself in my room and turned the music up loud. I thought Mum would get boozed after their argument, but she was up at seven this morning, vacuuming the floors. Early morning cleaning used to be a regular event, but the vacuum cleaner has barely made it out of the cupboard since Liam died. This morning the house is spotless.

When I go into the living room, Mum is smoothing already smooth cushions. I move to the window. I want to get a look at Siân before I meet her. I've talked to her on the phone and she sounds OK. I picture her middle-aged, boring, sensibly dressed and hard as nails. You'd have to be to do this kind of job.

"Are you all right?" Mum asks.

I wonder what part of today could possibly qualify me for being all right, but I force a smile. I've almost forgotten about the mum who cares whether or not I'm all right. She couldn't even begin to know. Her face, puffy and swollen earlier today, is now carefully made up. I wish I could talk to her, but Dad's made it clear that she can't deal with any more stress – which is his way of telling me to shut up when Mum's around. He's a fine one to talk.

Mum finds a tiny smear on the empty trophy cabinet and rushes off to get a duster. There's something sad about her determination to present the perfect home – to prove that she has no part in my criminal tendencies. *Don't worry, the guilt's all mine*, I'd like to say to her. But what's the point?

I pull the net curtain back a few centimetres to get a clearer view of the road. I have no idea what to expect from Siân or what she'll expect from me.

A car comes to a stop outside and Mum joins me at the window. For a moment the back of our hands touch and for some reason I apologize. It's bang on 10.30. The car door opens and I watch every move. This must be Siân, but she's nothing like I imagined. She's young and she's dressed in narrow jeans, canvas shoes, T-shirt and jacket. She's pretty too, her long, black hair twisted up into a clip at the back.

Mum rubs her hands up and down her skirt and walks towards the door. She has it open before Siân knocks. I hear them by the front door and I'm stunned by Mum's ability to rise to the occasion, another tiny glimpse of how she used to be.

Their voices move in my direction. It's only a

few steps. And now she's here, smiling, coming towards me with her hand held out to shake mine. It seems too friendly and I'm instantly on guard. My heart tells me to make myself as small and invisible as possible. My head tells me I must shake her hand.

She introduces herself and tells us both about what she does. She has a soft accent, from Ireland, she says, and a smile that lights up her face. She asks me how I'm getting on. I tell her I'm fine. Mum offers coffee or tea.

"Thank you," says Siân. "Tea if you're making it."

It would be easy to like this person, yet warnings fire off in my brain and I know I can't relax for a moment. I can't afford to slip into any traps and say something I shouldn't. I don't know what she knows. I don't know what's been going on *behind the scenes* as Dad likes to refer to it.

"Are you happy for us to talk in here?" she asks, indicating the chairs in the sitting room.

I nod.

"Would you like your mum here?"

"I'd prefer not if that's OK." If Siân has a view on this, she keeps it to herself.

"Shall we sit down then?" She puts her bag on the floor beside the armchair and perches on the edge of the seat. She indicates the next door chair for me to sit in. I feel like a guest in my own house.

Siân asks me how life has been since I was arrested and I tell her what I think she wants to hear: I'm back at work. Things are OK.

"For some people it can be quite a frightening and confusing time," she says in a way that sounds more like a question than a statement. It's an invitation to me to start talking, but I don't want to talk. She doesn't push me.

I listen to the sounds of Mum pulling mugs out of the cupboard in the kitchen and sliding the tray off the high shelf. She's even baked biscuits.

"Have you been seeing friends?" Siân asks.

I give a small shrug. "Some."

"And have you talked to them about what happened?"

"No, not really."

I'm not making this easy for her. She reaches into her bag and pulls out a file. It has a flowery cover. She doesn't open it, just puts it on the table.

"How's school been going? I suppose you had exams last term."

"Yeah. I haven't had my results yet."

She turns her mouth down at the corners. "Oh yes – results – I remember results days only too well! I'm sure you'll be fine."

I shrug.

"And I hear you're an excellent runner."

I wonder where all her information comes from. "My brother was the excellent runner," I say. "I'm pretty average."

There's a pause before Siân says, "I'm sorry about your brother. It must have been a hard year for you."

So she knows about Liam too.

"Have you had any counselling since he died?" she asks.

"No."

"Were you offered any?"

"Yep. At school. I didn't bother, though."

She nods and smiles again. "It's not for everyone," she says.

That makes me feel better.

Mum comes in with the tray of tea. Her hand shakes as she pours and her breath smells of extra-strong mints. It's a bad sign.

"We were just talking about running," Siân says to Mum.

Mum's gaze flickers towards the cabinet then back to me.

"I think Amber overdid the training a bit this year. Hopefully her knee will be mended for next season. Her dad's very keen. Liam was too."

"So Amber was saying."

Mum hardly ever mentions Liam's name in public and the pain is written on her face.

"Anyway, I'll leave you to it," she says, and scurries away.

Siân takes a sip of tea. "I'm sure you've had a chance to think a little more about what happened. About your part in the burglary."

I nod.

"Is there anything you'd like to ask me or tell me?"

"No." I say more aggressively than I mean to. I kick at the base of the chair with my heel. "I'd just like to know what's going to happen to me next. I thought that's what this meeting was about."

"Partly," she smiles. "I want you to know that I am here to help. That you can talk to me and ask me as many questions as you want."

"Thanks."

She pauses. Once again allowing me space to speak. I don't.

"As this is your first offence, and as you've owned up to your part in the burglary, it has been suggested you are given what's called a conditional caution."

"What does that mean?"

"It means you won't have to go to court or stand trial. As long as you can show us you are sorry for what you've done, and that you are prepared to take steps not to re-offend, no further action will be taken at this stage. Of course, it's also a warning. If you get into trouble again, you won't get off so lightly."

"So I just say sorry and that's it? No criminal record or anything?" There must be a catch somewhere.

"You won't get a criminal record, as such. However, a record will be kept on police files, which could be disclosed under certain circumstances – you know, certain jobs, that kind of thing."

"That's all?"

"Not quite." She pulls her file on to her lap and rests her hands on it. "We need to be sure that you understand the seriousness of what you've done. We'd like you to learn more about the effect your actions have had on the victims – on the people whose house was burgled."

"But I didn't go into the house."

"I realize that. But you were part of it and whether you were in the house or not doesn't necessarily make it any easier for the family. Is this something you've thought about?"

I hang my head. I haven't – not really. I was too far removed from it all. I've had too much else to think about. "No," I say. "I suppose not."

"We'd like you to think about it and that's what this meeting is about. Often hearing the other side of the story can help you to make better decisions in the future; help you not to make the same mistakes again."

"I've already said I'm sorry. I meant it. I know what I did was wrong."

"And the others who were involved? Do you think they know what they did was wrong? Would you be able to stand up to them if the situation arose again?" Her voice is still kind, not accusing. She doesn't push me.

Would I? If Declan was there with a knife – would I stand up to him? This is stuff I have to work out. Am I kidding myself that if I say nothing, no one else will get hurt and Declan will go away and never come back again?

"Have you ever heard of restorative justice?" she asks.

I shake my head. Siân puts down her cup and settles herself back in her chair. "A restorative justice conference is when we arrange for you to meet with the victim of your crime. Both of you have to agree to the meeting. It gives you the chance to hear how your actions have affected him and his family and you also get the chance to explain your side of the story. We will try and help you both towards an outcome that can help you move on."

I try to process this idea in my head, pushing the thought this way and that.

"Why would he want to meet me? After what I've done?"

"That's a good question and not easy to answer. It often helps the victim to understand more about why the offender did what they did and to understand you as a person. Sometimes it can help to take away the fear."

"Whose fear?"

"The victim's."

I nod. Not mine then. No such luck.

"We prepare for these meetings very carefully.

I'd be there with you and you can choose someone to bring with you to support you. It could be your mum, perhaps, or your dad."

I shake my head. I don't want Mum or Dad with me.

"Would I have to answer a lot of questions again?"

Siân seems to know, instinctively, what I'm talking about.

"I know there are things that it's difficult for you to talk about. You don't have to say anything you don't want to say. It's hard to predict exactly how these meetings will go, and they are not always easy, but they really do give you an opportunity to make a difference – both to yourself and to the victim. I'd like you to at least consider it."

"Could I have Gran with me?"

"You can have whoever you want, within reason!" She laughs, opens the file for the first time and makes a note. Then she flicks on a couple of pages and I watch her eyes run down the page.

"Am I right in saying your grandmother hasn't been well? How is she?"

"She's getting better. She's home now."

"That's good. I'm glad. And she lives nearby?"

I'm certain Siân already knows the answer to this. She seems to know a lot about me – but I nod anyway.

"Do you think she'd be happy to support you; that she'd be up to it?"

"Depends when this meeting will be," I say. "She's getting stronger every day. Yeah, I think she'd like to be there with me."

"I'll need to talk to your grandmother. Are you happy for me to do that?"

"Yes," I say again. "Can I tell her first though?"

"Of course."

She gives me a card with all her contact details and we make a time for the next meeting.

"If you have any questions, just call me. I may not be able to take your call straight away but I will always ring you back. Is there anything else you want to discuss before I go?"

"I don't think so."

We finish our tea and Siân asks me about my interests. I say I like cooking and movies and she says she could do with a few cake-baking lessons. She's probably not interested in baking at all, but it's the kind of thing you say when you want to be friendly. And I do like her – she's OK.

"Shall we take this out to the kitchen?" Siân

stands and picks up the tray. She carries it through to the kitchen and has another quick chat to Mum before she leaves.

The minute the door closes, I expect Mum to want to know everything that's happened. Instead, she tells me she's feeling very tired. She asks me if I'd mind *holding the fort* at Gran's. I guess Mum's overheard most of our conversation anyway. Our house is hardly soundproof.

"I'm not going to be sent to prison," I say and Mum nods. "I don't even have to go to court."

She gives the smallest smile. "That's a relief then. I think I'll go up for a rest." I recognize the look in her eyes, the desperation for oblivion, and I watch her climb towards it stair by stair.

"But it's *good* news Mum. We could go together to Gran's. Celebrate."

She keeps walking. Hopelessness pulls at my stomach. I wish I could show her there's another way. She's held everything together so well over the last few weeks. I suppose it couldn't last for ever. Still, I wish it wasn't me that sent her racing back to the bottle.

I wash up the tea things and think about Siân. It wasn't nearly as bad as I expected. All I have to do is meet the victim. Will he hate me? I stare into the bubbles and watch the tiny rainbows of light. I remember how I felt when the boys were all standing, uninvited, in my kitchen – how I'm scared to leave a window open now. Is this how he feels too? Violated? Scared?

I can't do this without Gran. I need to make sure she'll come with me. I empty the sink, grab my things and leave the house. I know I should've checked on Mum, but some things are too hard. If I don't see, I can pretend I don't know.

CHAPTER 20

Gran is pottering in her kitchen when I arrive. It's incredible how quickly she's back on her feet. She wants to hear all about the meeting with Siân and I tell her every last detail.

"Well," she says, "that all sounds very sensible and, of course, I'm honoured that you'd like me to support you." She puts her arm around me. "Did you really have to ask?"

"I thought it might be too much for you?"

"Strong as an ox," she says. "Albeit rather an old ox who could do with sitting down!"

I help Gran to her chair.

"You know what you said about making peace with myself? Do you think this might be it? Having this meeting with the victim?"

I push Gran's footstool towards her and lift her feet on to it.

"Who knows," says Gran. "You'll have to wait and see what happens."

It's the waiting that's the worst. I didn't think this would be such a hard thing to do. But it makes you think a lot about the kind of person you are – and I don't like the person I am. The more I talk to Siân, the closer to the meeting I get, the more I'm forced to confront the fact that Declan is still a threat, and not just to me. For all I know, they could be watching me this very minute or they could be breaking into another person's house, creating another victim. Are there a whole load of other people like me out there – people too scared to speak out?

Mum's on a downer. I know it's my fault; Dad doesn't need to keep reminding me how my situation *makes things very difficult* for my mother. It doesn't make things very easy for me either, but *she* is allowed not to cope and each day I resent it a little more.

I've talked to Dad about the restorative justice conference and he listened. He's pleased I don't have to go to court. I avoid telling him about Gran coming with me until the last minute. I didn't think he'd care that much, but I'm wrong.

"I don't think you appreciate how much we do for you, Amber. We could've thrown you out, you know?"

I feel like I should be grateful. I wish he was the dad that I did want to have with me, that I did appreciate. "You're never here to meet Siân," I say. It's easier than trying to explain. "You're always at work. And I thought it would be too stressful for Mum."

He gives a kind of hmmph. "This restorative justice thing – it all sounds like trendy twaddle to me anyway," he says.

"It's what I have to do, Dad, like it or not."

Clearly, he does not like it and yet, when the day arrives, he takes the day off to drive Gran and me to the meeting. Perhaps he's determined to show who is boss, or determined to show that he can control this process in some way. He isn't and he can't. On the way there he keeps making comments about how I should prepare myself for a right grilling. The last thing I want to do is discuss any part of this with Dad. The atmosphere in the car reminds me of driving to running competitions. I'm surprised Dad doesn't slide in his favourite CD and play "We are the Champions" over and over; as if this is some kind of competition between me and the victim.

Gran must see the effect Dad's having on me because she stops him mid-sentence. "Amber knows what to expect," she says. "Siân has explained everything and perhaps it is better if neither of us interferes."

Dad's face turns red. I can see he's bursting to answer back, but he must think better of it. I wind down my window a crack and feel the thin stream of air on my face. The closer we get, the more I want to run away. Dad slows in the final stretch of road as he searches for the right building and then a parking space.

"Come on," says Gran, giving me a shove, "imagination is usually far worse than reality." I get out and then help Gran on to the pavement. She takes my arm and we walk together towards the meeting place. "Remember what I told you. This is your chance to put things right and you should count yourself very lucky. You'll feel better when it's all over."

When, I think to myself. *When* it's all over. It hasn't even started yet. I picture Dad watching us walk away. Maybe he just wanted to be here to witness my humiliation.

Siân is waiting for us. "Are you ready, Amber?"

I need the toilet badly. Nerves. Siân shows me where to go. I use the time alone to try to breathe. To get my head clear.

"OK." I take a breath and puff it out audibly. I take another. And another. "OK," I say again. I tell myself over and over that this guy waiting in the conference room can't do anything to me. *Come on*, I tell myself. *Come on.*

I splash a little water on to my face and dry it with a paper towel, then return to Siân and Gran and we go into a room where he is already waiting. His gaze is so direct that I'd reverse straight back out again if Gran wasn't standing behind me. I turn my eyes to the floor, a nasty mustard-coloured carpet. I am the offender, he is the victim. I don't feel like an offender. I feel like it should be the other way round. I try to get an idea of what he's like without looking at his face. His shoes are polished, his trousers smart. Money.

I sit down, my back to the door and Gran sits next to me. Siân takes her place at the end of the table and starts to speak.

"I'd like to welcome everybody here today and thank you all very much for coming. I appreciate that this may not be easy for any of you. As you all know, my name is Siân."

She smiles at each one of us.

"This is Amber and this is Ruby, Amber's grandmother."

We sound like a jewellery shop. My leg jitters up and down and I can't make it stop. Gran puts her hand out and tries to steady it. It doesn't work.

"And this is Dr Levine."

I force myself to meet his eyes for a moment and he gives a small nod. I wonder why he hasn't brought anyone with him. Maybe he doesn't need anyone to support him. Maybe he's got no friends or family. I'm sure Siân mentioned family in one of our conversations.

"During this meeting we'll look at what happened earlier this month at Dr Levine's house. It is important to understand that the focus of the meeting will be on Amber's actions and how these have affected others, specifically Dr Levine and his family."

I see Dr Levine rub one of his eyes. So he has got family.

"As you know, none of you are here to decide

whether anybody is a good or bad person. You are here to explore how people have been affected by what has happened, and hopefully for all of you to work towards repairing the harm that was caused." She goes on to explain that we must respect each other and that we have to take it in turns to talk; that we will each be given the chance to have our say and to ask questions. I've been told all this already, in our preparatory meetings at home, but I try to listen carefully so I don't get anything wrong.

"Normally, at this point, I would ask you to check that your mobile phones are switched off. However, Dr Levine has asked to be allowed to keep his on for personal reasons. Is that all right with you?" Siân looks towards Gran and me. I wonder what his personal reasons are. Gran nods. I shrug.

"Perhaps we could start by looking at what you all hope to get out of this meeting. Amber, would you like to start?"

I would not like to start even though I've rehearsed this a thousand times. My mouth is dry as cardboard. I look to Gran for support and she gives my hand a small squeeze.

"I want to tell Dr Levine that I'm sorry for what I did – for the part I played in the burglary. I want him to understand that there were some reasons I did it, but now I know those reasons were the wrong reasons."

I say my whole speech to the table and I stick to the script. It makes it sound insincere. In the silence that follows I force myself to look up. Dr Levine is kind of smiling at me. There's doubt there, for sure, but his eyes are kind.

"Thank you," he says, "for your apology. I hope you don't mind if I ask you some questions."

My eyes flick towards Siân and she indicates that I should let him continue.

"First, I'd like you to tell me exactly what part you played. Most of all, I'd like to know why? Why us? We've never done anything to hurt anyone. What did we do that made you pick us out? What did we do to deserve it?"

That's a lot of questions and in the short silence that follows, it strikes me that I'm not the one with the answers. In fact I could ask the very same questions: Why did Declan, Joel and Tyler pick me? What did I do to deserve it?

"Amber, perhaps you could tell Dr Levine exactly what happened," says Siân, prompting me to say something.

I outline, as best I can, what happened on that afternoon. It's all a bit garbled — not what I intended and the unfairness of it hammers in my chest. I want him to know that I never actually went into his house. It wasn't me who stole his stuff.

Was it planned in advance he wants to know? Had someone been watching his house and knew when the house was empty? He seems to be getting more worked up with each question.

I try to think. "I'm not sure. Maybe. I think they'd scouted the area before."

"You say *they* so not you?"

I shake my head.

"Anyone watching our house would know it's empty a lot of the time. I suppose that makes us an easy target." He rubs his thumb against the tip of his forefinger as he thinks. "But that still doesn't make it right, does it? I mean what gave you the right to make our life worse than it already is?"

I'm shaking my head. He should try living my life. What would he say if he knew about Liam and Mum and Tyler and Declan? He hasn't got a clue. Whatever he's seeing when he looks at me is wrong — it's not the real me.

Siân starts to speak, but he stops her. "I'm sorry," he says, clasping his hands together. I watch him regain control. "I think it might help Amber to know something about my family – if that's all right."

I can hardly say no.

"Whatever your reasons for doing what you did," he speaks to me directly now, "it might help you to understand how deeply your actions have affected us. It may have been totally unintentional on your behalf, but I believe you need to know so that next time – well, so there won't *be* a next time."

I bite my bottom lip. I don't think I'm going to like what I'm about to hear. I'm not sure I've got anywhere else to go with my guilt. It'd be easier not to know, but I'm not going to have that luxury. Dr Levine is already speaking.

"I have two teenage children, not far off your age. We moved to our house about three months ago to be nearer to the hospital."

The word *hospital* makes me focus harder.

"Our son, Jeremy, is very sick." Dr Levine stops to clear his throat and take a few breaths. "He's waiting for a heart transplant. If a heart doesn't become available soon, he may not survive. I suppose you could say he's living on borrowed time."

I try to shut out the words. The memories of Liam are too close. I can almost feel him sitting on my shoulder. And Gran is silent beside me. She and Jeremy could've been in the same ward.

"My wife spent a lot of time making our new home a special place for us to be, a place for Jeremy to come home to on the rare occasions when he is allowed out of hospital. You've destroyed all that. Someone even threw eggs at the walls. I can understand why people want to take things, but why would they throw eggs?"

It's such a small, insignificant thing. Eggs. Yet this is what he chooses to focus on. Destruction for destruction's sake.

I press the palms of my hands into my eyes to try to black out the pictures in my head.

"Since it happened, my wife and daughter are scared to go home, scared even to open a window. Every time we walk into the house, we relive the memory of that day. Every time we walk out, we wonder what might happen while we're not there. Who is watching?" His fingers are tapping fast on the table. "We were barely coping as it was. Now it's almost unbearable. If you'd knocked on the door and asked me for money or whatever else you wanted, I would've given to you. Anything rather than this."

"But I didn't want anything," I say shaking my head.

He frowns into a long silence. "You're telling me you just did it for fun?"

"NO! I did it because *I* was scared – and a bit drunk."

Dr Levine flops back in his chair. If only I could really explain. I know about hearts and death and fear. I know how he feels. I do. Except I'm somehow responsible for his suffering and for his family's too. We are on opposite sides of the table, opposite sides of the law. If I hadn't been with the boys that day, would they have gone ahead? If only they'd chosen a different house – any other house. Siân said this meeting would help. I don't think it's helping any of us. I can't change what's happened. I can't make him understand. I can't do anything. And that's wrong. That's not fair.

"Amber," says Siân. "Is there anything you would like to say to Dr Levine?"

There's everything I'd like to say, but I don't

know how to say it or even *if* to say it. No one tries to prompt me this time. I hadn't planned for this. Do I tell my story? Will it make a difference or will it make things worse? I can see Gran's fingers. She's twisting her wedding ring round and round. Her foot edges towards mine, as if she's trying to kick me to get me started.

"My brother died a year ago. He was eighteen. He had a heart attack while he was out running with a friend." I tell it in a flat voice, like it's the dullest story you've ever heard. I don't want him to feel sorry for me. "It's been difficult – for everyone. I never meant to get into trouble. I was stupid and got involved with the wrong group of people. I didn't know anything about what they were going to do to your house until right before it happened. I had to do what I was told. I didn't want to. Then I got caught. And now I'm here and I'm very sad for your son and what I've done to your family and I wish there was something I could do. But I can't change what's happened. It's too late."

I don't feel like I've said what I want to say, but it's hard to pick the right words.

Dr Levine has his face in his hands. Slowly, he slides his hands downwards, pulling the skin as he goes, draining the last remaining colour from his cheeks.

Siân allows time for everyone to settle. It's all so hopeless.

"Ruby," Siân says, looking at Gran. "Is there anything you would like to add?"

"Only that I know my granddaughter is not a bad person. She's a family girl, a bright girl and a kind girl. She's never been in trouble before. She's had a rough ride for the last year and there are a number of us to blame for that, myself included. If I hadn't encouraged Amber to get out a bit more, I don't think she'd have got herself into this situation. But she did and we can't turn back the clock. Thank you, Dr Levine, for giving Amber the chance to meet you and for telling us about your family. I think all of us here have had more than our fair share of misfortune. Perhaps we all have something to learn from this. I can only hope that the outcome for your son is good."

I love Gran. She can say things so they sound right.

Next, Siân turns to Dr Levine. "Is there anything you would like Amber to do to help make amends for what has happened?"

Amends is a stupid word. What can I do to make amends? I can't make a difference to this family. I can't undead Liam, unmeet Tyler and Declan and Joel or unburgle the Levine's house. I can't work a miracle for their son and make everything better. Nothing I do will change anything for them or for me.

Dr Levine interlaces his fingers and stares at his hands. Then he pulls his fingers apart and places the tips together in a steeple. I wait to hear what my *amending* will involve.

"I am very, very sorry to hear about your brother. I mean that. I appreciate you telling me and I'm sure life hasn't been easy for you. But you still have a good chance at life and I don't want you to waste that." Out of the corner of my eye, I can see Gran nodding. "Getting into trouble and making other people's lives miserable is not the answer. It's not going to help anyone – least of all you. I'd like you to think very hard about what you have done and the way it has affected us, and you, and your family as well. I think I can understand why you can't, or won't, name the other people involved, but you have to realize they're still out there. They'll find other girls like you to prey on. They'll hurt other people – people like us. You have choices you can make. All I'm asking is that you make the right choices."

We had a talk once, at school, on choices. Choices, we were told, give us power. So we have to be careful what we do with those choices. So far my record hasn't been good. Gran stretches over and gently pulls my fingers away from my mouth. I suppose I'm chewing my nails – what's left of them.

"Will your son get a new heart?" I ask. It's all I can think about.

"I wish I could answer that question," says Dr Levine. "There are a lot of people waiting and there are never enough donors. At some point, he'll get one, I suppose. It's whether or not he gets one in time."

"He can have mine."

Dr Levine laughs. "That's a generous offer, but I don't think it would be very practical."

I look at him and see that he really is laughing. To begin with, I can't work out why. Then I get it. What a stupid thing to say – that I'll give him my heart. The tension suddenly breaks and I can't help but smile too. How can we be laughing about something so serious? How can we be laughing together? This is crazy.

But something in the room has changed and an idea has already begun to form in my mind.

I sense a possibility and I do want to make amends – to everyone. Maybe Gran's right. Maybe there is a way.

CHAPTER 21

The traffic is bad as we head towards the hospital. What had I expected to come out of my meeting with Dr Levine? Not this, for sure; not to be going to visit a critically ill 18-year-old. This will be my third visit to this hospital – not counting the time I was born. First Liam, then Gran, now Jeremy. Lucky number three? Simon has come with me. I didn't ask him to, but he offered and I'm glad of the company and support. He's kept to his promise and I've kept to mine. He's chatty all the way in the car, trying to keep my mind off things. He comes with me as far as the lift then says he'll wait in the cafeteria.

I take the lift to the fifth floor. High dependency.

Dr Levine comes out to meet me. He shakes my hand. "I'll take you in," he says, "but you can only visit for a short time."

I nod. I don't think I want to be here for long.

Gran's warned me about all the tubes and wires and she's not wrong. *Think of it as a recording studio,* she said, *it's easier that way.* I don't know how on earth Gran knows anything about recording studios, but I keep her words in my head. Anything to keep my mind away from hospital and death and Liam. If he'd survived, would he have ended up here? In this ward stacked with monitors, machines and never-ending bleeps? I'd expected individual rooms; I was wrong.

I was wrong about Jeremy too. I'd imagined someone barely conscious, weak, I don't know — at the very least a rather pathetic person lying helpless in the bed. Of course, he *is* in a bed, and he's thin and pale, but his eyes are alert and alive and his smile is incredible.

"So you're the infamous Amber," he says and waves vaguely at the banks of monitors and machines stacked around his bed. "Welcome to the world of *Big Brother!*"

His choice of words couldn't be worse, even though I know they have nothing to do with Liam.

"Hi," I say.

"You can go now, Dad," he says.

Dr Levine grins. "Thanks. I know when I'm not wanted."

I'm not sure I want Dr Levine to go.

"Have a seat, but whatever you do, don't kick that container over." Jeremy indicates something on the floor by his bedside. I have to stop myself from making a bad face as I look at the colour of the contents. I sit down carefully.

"I've never talked to a real-life burglar before," he continues. He sounds serious, but I can tell from his eyes he is laughing at me and it makes me self-conscious. "You don't exactly look how I imagined – you know, stripy shirt, pair of tights over your head, that kind of thing."

"Sorry to disappoint you," I say. "I thought I should change before coming to visit or they might not let me in."

"True," he grins. "Don't worry. Dad's told me you're OK. I hope he was nice to you – in your big meeting."

I'm surprised by Jeremy's openness. Not one for small talk, it would appear.

"Considering what the meeting was about, yeah, he was very nice. I was hardly expecting him to like me."

"Perhaps one does not want to be loved so much as to be understood." Jeremy says this in a theatrical way and I wonder what he is talking about.

"Sorry?"

"A quote from *1984*. I've just finished reading it for about the eighth time."

Jeremy picks up the book from his side table and hands it to me. "Have you read it?" he asks.

"No. I haven't."

"You should. It's good. Take it if you like."

"I can't do that."

"That's funny coming from a burglar!" He laughs. "Oh well, if you don't want to steal it you can take it as a present."

"I'd rather you stopped calling me a burglar."

"It sounds so much more exciting than an accessory."

"You could try Amber."

He laughs. "Nah – I prefer Accessory. You should choose your friends more carefully. Apparently they stitched you up. That's what Dad told me."

"Did he? I was stupid."

"You don't look stupid."

I shrug, embarrassed. "Thanks."

"The only bit of you that strikes me as stupid is

the bit that that won't tell the police the names of the others involved."

"I didn't really come here to talk about that," I say. He ignores me.

"I sort of admire you for your loyalty," he goes on, "but I'm still working it out in my head. I know things are rarely as simple as they seem. I suppose one of them was your boyfriend or something?"

My cheeks burn. Was he? I hate the fact that Tyler still has such a hold on me.

"I'm right!" says Jeremy, studying my face.

"No, you're not. I don't have a boyfriend."

"But you did? And now, after what happened, you don't see him any more."

"No." It comes out sounding defensive.

"Ambiguous. I like ethical issues, they fascinate me. I never used to give them a second thought but things change and I've got an overload of spare time now — to lie around and think. It's ironic really."

He moves slightly in the bed and, for the first time, I can see the effort and pain on his face.

"Dad says you offered to personally donate your heart to me. Not the brightest idea on the planet, but a kind thought."

I wonder if Jeremy is always like this. It's hard to know when he's being serious and when he's not.

"If it makes you feel better, I wouldn't want your heart anyway. You're far too small, for a start. And far too pretty." I blush. "Even prettier when you blush."

"Jeremy!" says his nurse in a warning voice as he leans out from behind a screen at the bottom of the bed. I'd almost forgotten anyone else was with us. "Give the poor girl a break — not all of us are used to your questionable sense of humour."

"I'm not trying to be funny," he says, and puts on the most wide-eyed, innocent face possible. Then he laughs again. "When you're in my position, you don't worry too much about what you say or what people think."

"I guess."

"Dad says you want to launch a campaign for more organ donors."

"Yes. I've decided I wanted to do something to help. You know, to try to—"

"I don't want you to do this for me, Amber."

I'm stunned. Disappointed. "Why?"

"I don't know. A lot of reasons. To save me, someone else has to die. Someone else's family has to go through the misery my family could go through. Sometimes, I'm not sure how I feel about that. I just don't want it to be personal, that's all."

"Yes, but you don't cause their death, do you? They don't die because you need their heart. They die anyway. It happens. I should know."

"Dad told me about your brother. I'm sorry."

"Liam was the same age as you. I know his heart wasn't any good but, apart from that, he was fit and healthy. He could have donated other organs, but he wasn't a registered donor. I think it would have helped us – to know that his death wasn't a waste and that something good could come out of it. I think Liam would have wanted that too, if he'd ever stopped to think about it. But you don't think about dying when you're young, do you?"

Jeremy smiles a tired smile.

"Not unless you're sick," I add quickly. "All the people I run with are fit and healthy. I just want to encourage them to think. It's too late for Liam, but it's not too late for them – and it's not too late for you."

"I don't want to let you down, Amber."

"What do you mean?"

He looks away from me. "You know. If I don't. . .

I wouldn't like you to think it was your fault."

"All I want is to do something to make it up to your family," I say.

"You don't need to. The only thing Dad wants is to make sure you don't mess up your own life."

"I've already done that – and a few other people's for good measure. I'm trying to unmess it all."

"So you're doing this for you then – not just us."

I think for a moment. "Maybe. Gran calls it a way of making peace with myself."

"That's OK then. That's a good reason. Do you mind if I ask you something?"

"Depends what it is!"

Jeremy looks very serious.

"Do you feel guilty because you're alive and your brother is dead?"

I pause. I know the answer, but I'm not sure what answer I should give Jeremy – or if I should answer at all.

"Honestly?" I say and he nods. "Every day."

He looks sad. "It's something I've been wondering. It's going to be hard for my little sister if anything happens to me. I'm trying to understand what it is like to be the one left. I want to write her a letter, just in case. Do you think that's a good idea?"

I try to imagine what it would be like if Liam had left me a letter. If he'd had the chance. . .

"You're not going to die," I say.

A machine starts beeping and I watch the nurse as he quickly makes some adjustments. "Now look what you've done." Jeremy closes his eyes. "You've got the machinery all worked up."

"I'm sorry," I stammer. I watch the nurse looking up at the various screens until the bleeping subsides. It's easy to forget the reality of this situation.

"Bowl," he says to the nurse.

"Shall I go?" I'm not sure what I did to cause this, but I should definitely leave. I've been here too long already.

"No don't. Just give me a minute. I feel sick when my heart goes into orbit. Hopefully I won't actually vomit – not after practising all my chat-up lines."

I hope he doesn't vomit too – though I'm quite used to it with Mum. We sit in silence and I watch Jeremy's pale fingers curl and uncurl against the edge of the cardboard bowl. After a short while he pushes it away and I relax a little.

"Dad says you'd like my help with your campaign." He's looking exhausted now. "I'm afraid I can't take part in a fun run or anything like that."

I smile. "A marathon perhaps?! No, all I want is permission to mention your name. It's the opening meeting of the running club coming up and I'm planning a presentation. I want to persuade as many people as possible so sign up as donors. The club are keen to support me because my brother used to be their best runner."

"So this'll be for him too. I'm beginning to get it now."

"Your dad has asked that I use the opportunity to tell my own story – how I came to meet you. He thinks it will help other young people. So I wanted to ask you if you'd mind if I talk about you in my presentation. That's all."

"Dad's asked you to talk about how you got into trouble? That'll be tough, won't it?"

"Yes, I guess it will, and my dad will probably freak out. But I want to do it."

"As long as you mention that I'm witty and good-looking then I'm cool with the rest." He barely has the energy to laugh.

The nurse smiles at me. "I think Jeremy needs to rest now," he says.

I look at my watch. "Oh, God, I'm sorry. I didn't mean to stay this long. Your dad said only five minutes." I get up, almost forgetting to be careful where I put my feet.

He shakes his head. "Don't go."

"I'm sure Amber's had quite enough of you for one day," says the nurse. Jeremy holds one finger up at him and he laughs.

"Will you come again?" He can barely keep his eyes open.

As I tiptoe away I hear him whisper, "Good luck."

"Good luck to you too," I whisper back. But I don't think he hears.

CHAPTER 22

I'm not going to let him die.

If Jeremy survives then everything will be all right. That's what I've told myself; somehow, it will all sort itself out. I don't know how – I don't need to know how. Saving Jeremy has become an obsession. How hard can it be? This is how I can make it up to Dr Levine and Liam and Gran and Mum and Dad and anyone else whose lives I've messed up.

I don't have long. I can't spend months planning and preparing because Jeremy may not have months. Dad can't get his head round it at all. He keeps asking if it's some form of community service. His main concern is that I don't make a fool of myself – or perhaps him – in front of all the members of the running club. I've told him about the organ donation bit but I haven't mentioned that I'm going to talk about how I got involved with the police. If he knew about that, he'd stop me, for sure.

Meeting Jeremy has made me stronger. If he can be brave and cheerful and positive then I can too. I hold on to that. I know Declan and Tyler are still out there and Declan's threats are still real. I've kept my mouth shut and if they will only leave me alone, at least until I've done this, that's all I ask.

And then? Then I have some decisions to make. But for now I push that aside because I'm working out that some things are worth fighting for and some aren't. Jeremy's easy – I'll fight for him all the way. As for the rest, I haven't made up my mind yet.

Standing in the corner of the sports hall, I watch as people start to arrive. There are a lot of faces I know, and many I don't. In less than an hour, I'm going to have to stand up in front of all of them and give my presentation. Talking in public is not something I do – ever, let alone when I'm going to talk about Liam, about Jeremy, about why they should become organ donors. I'd like to run away, but if I've learnt anything over the past few months, it's that running away never works. Will anybody listen to me?

Simon comes up and puts his arm around me.

"OK?"

"I'm not sure I can do this."

"Too late to change your mind now."

I hang my head miserably.

"Hey, come on," he says punching my arm. "Your speech is great."

"What if no one signs up? What if Jeremy doesn't survive?"

"You can't think like that. Even if you only get one new donor it'll be a bonus. Stop moping around and remind yourself why you're doing this. You said Jeremy didn't want it to be about him and it isn't. Not really."

"Perhaps you'd like to do the speech for me, since you're so confident."

"I don't have the necessary criminal qualifications," says Simon with a smile. "Liam wasn't my brother and I don't know Jeremy. Apart from that, no problem."

I watch as people edge their way into the rows

of seats, ready for the meeting. There's a mixture of parents, teenagers and young kids, new to the running club. There's always a rush at the start of the season and then a lot drop out.

The president calls everyone to order and the crowded hall gradually goes quiet. I pretend to look interested as he explains how things are going to work this year. It's the same as it works every year so I don't know why he bothers. The usual parents ask the usual stupid questions and the usual moaners moan. I keep unfolding, reading, and refolding my speech. I wish they'd all shut up so I can get this over and done with.

Finally there are no more hands left in the air, no more questions to be asked. The president stands up.

"Now, before you all go, one of our members would like to say a few words. Amber, would you like to come to the front?"

If this is what it means to make amends, then I'm beginning to understand how hard it is. A ripple of chatter starts as I take my place. I clear my throat but no one takes any notice. I fix Jeremy in my mind, and Liam. A small chorus of "shhhhhhs" circles the audience.

My hands shake as I unfold my speech. I try to remember all the things Gran has told me about talking to the back of the hall. Here goes.

"Hello," I start but my voice barely comes out. I look at my feet. I try again.

"Hello," I say to the back of the hall. "As most of you know my name is Amber Neville. I've been a member of this club for five years. . ." The hall seems very large and I make my voice as loud as I can. "In a moment I am going to show you a short film about organ donation, but first of all I am going to tell you why I'm here."

I force myself to look around the room, to engage with my audience.

That's when I see him. There, leaning against the wall in the corner by the door. Tyler Dawson. The sight of him knocks the breath out of me. How stupid could I be? Of course this is where he'd find me. No one can question him being here; he's a club member after all. He's wearing his tracksuit with the hood up and his club T-shirt. He knows I'm looking at him. His head is down but his eyes are lifted, watching me. My emotions splinter. I'm scared, I'm angry, I want to scream at him to go away, and yet. . .

A small child near the front whines, "Has she finished?" I take a deep breath. Fuck you, Tyler Dawson, I think. I'm not giving up now.

"My brother Liam was eighteen years old and fit and healthy – or that's what we thought. You'll find his name on just about every trophy in the club – except for the girls' ones, of course." There's some laughter and that helps. "Just over a year ago, as some of you know, Liam died suddenly and unexpectedly of catastrophic heart failure." The atmosphere in the room changes. You can feel it – see it in the way people move slightly in their seats. "The effect on my family was devastating." My voice cracks and I fight to regain control. "I think we all went a bit off the rails; Mum, Dad and me, but me especially. We all blamed ourselves. We all wondered if there was something we should, or could have done. Sometimes tragedy brings out the best in people and sometimes the worst. In our family, it's brought out the worst." I look at Dad, but he is staring at the floor. I swallow. "In my case, I ended up hanging out with the wrong people—" I risk a glance towards Tyler "—and I ended up in trouble with the police." He's still as a stone. Him and Dad. There are some murmurs from the audience, some shuffling. "I was involved in a burglary on a house— a house belonging to Dr and Mrs Levine, their daughter and their son, Jeremy. Obviously, I didn't know them at the time but I met Dr Levine in a restorative justice conference – a meeting where victims and offenders get together to talk." The lines of faces watch me expectantly. A baby starts crying. I need to keep going. "That's how I got to hear about Jeremy. He is eighteen, the same age as Liam was when he died. Jeremy has a serious heart condition and is waiting for a transplant. If he doesn't get a new heart soon – very soon – he may not survive." I'm into my stride now. I can do this.

"Did you know that over a thousand people die every year while waiting for organ transplants? That's about three every day." There are murmurs of surprise. "If Jeremy doesn't get a transplant soon, he will become one of those three. He will die because there aren't enough donors. I want to change that." The atmosphere in the room has changed again. Dad is looking at me now and he's nodding. "For me, this is a very personal campaign. I'm doing it because I want to show Jeremy, his family, my family and the whole community how sorry I am for what

I've done. All of us are young and fit and I hope that none of us is going to die any time soon. But if the worst happens – like it did to my brother – then each and every one of us could help to save another life: in fact many lives. It means our death wouldn't be a complete waste. Liam wasn't a donor but I know he would have become one if he'd lived long enough to think about it. So I'm asking all of you to think about it and to ask your friends and family to think about it."

I have to pause. Suddenly all the emotions of the last few months, of the last year, are exploding inside me.

"I'm doing this for Jeremy and for Liam and I'm asking you to help me. Thank you."

I choke out the last few words and stumble off the stage. I hear clapping. The screen at the front blazes with colour as Simon sets the short campaign film going. It's only a couple of minutes long. I move quietly along the side of the hall in semi-darkness, to where Tyler was standing. I'm safe with all these people around me.

He's gone.

I scan the room, but there's no sign of him. I want to know why he was here. Everyone is now focused on the screen at the front. At the end, the lights go up and the president brings the meeting back to order. He thanks me, peering out to see where I've gone, and directs everyone who would like to sign up to the tables at the back of the hall. This is what it's about and yet my focus has shifted. Tyler fills my head.

A man with a notebook pushes in beside me and he tells me he's from the local paper. He'd like more details so he can run a full story. Another person snaps my photograph. There are questions. Already I can see people lining up. I can see people talking to Dad and Dad smiling as if all this was his idea. People congratulate me as they pass. They tell me I'm brave for telling my story.

Adrenaline is racing and all the time my eyes keep searching the room. Gran handing out supporter bracelets. The headteacher of a local school asks me if I'll do a talk in assembly next term and two other people ask if I'll speak at their sports clubs. Everything inside me starts to buzz. This could work.

But where is Tyler?

My eyes fix on the exit door. I know he's out there, waiting. I can feel it. And I know I have to see him. I pose with the club president as he shakes my hand and more photos are taken.

"Will you be running this season?" he asks me.

"I hope so. I'm working on my fitness." I pause, trying to get the right tone. "I think I saw Tyler Dawson here. Do you know if he's signed up for this year?"

The president smiles. "He has indeed. It'll be good to have him back. He was one of our top runners – along with your brother, of course."

What game is Tyler playing? What is he doing? I excuse myself, say I need some air.

Simon stops me on my way to the door. "It's OK, you can smile now," he says. "That was brilliant."

I try to look enthusiastic. "Back in a moment," I say. Luckily the toilets are near the entrance and they provide a good alibi. I walk into the ladies, wait a couple of seconds, then slip outside. The evening air is cool and I walk slowly down the steps and lean against the wall.

Within seconds, I hear a loud whisper.

"Amber?"

His voice makes my heart stop. This must be the most stupid thing I've ever done. What if Simon is right and all this is a trick? What if Declan is waiting round the corner? There are still plenty of people milling around. I can shout for help if I need it.

"I'm on my own," he says, coming closer, talking quietly. His hood is up and his head is down so I can't really see his face. "It's safe. You don't need to worry. I need to talk to you." He stretches out his hand, but I don't take it. I follow him away from the entrance, away from the lights.

"That's far enough," I say.

"Are you all right?" he asks.

"How can you even ask me that?"

"It was a good speech." He still doesn't look at me. "Liam would've liked it."

"Don't tell me what my brother would or wouldn't like. What are you doing here?" I ask.

He looks up and I see the bruising round his eyes, across the bridge of his nose. It wasn't obvious in the hall, but it is now, close up.

"Tyler! What happened?"

"The police came asking questions."

"It wasn't me, I promise," I say backing away. "I didn't say anything to the police."

"But I did," he says. "I turned myself in and I've told them everything."

"You did what? Are you mad? Now what's going to happen?"

Tyler pulls up his sweatshirt so I can see the bruises across his chest and stomach. *This,* his eyes scream at me. *THIS already happened.* He's badly beaten up.

"Declan?"

"Of course Declan." He spits out the name.

"How do I know you're telling the truth?"

"You think I'd beat myself up? I'm not that thick. You'll have to trust me on this one."

"Trust you?" My voice is too loud.

He drops his shirt, shakes his head. "I've got to see you. Properly. Not here. I need to talk to you."

"No."

"I've told you. I've turned myself in. And the others."

"How come you're here and not banged up in a police cell somewhere?"

"I'm on bail until I appear in court."

"And the others?"

"Joel and Becky have talked. Declan's up to his neck in it. I guess you'll be called as a witness."

I lean against the wall. I don't want to be part

of this. I don't want any more trouble. I want to draw a line under what's happened and move on.

"You have to leave me alone," I say.

"I can't. Not yet. We're in this together. I owe you an explanation, at least."

I sigh with frustration. Tyler scuffs the ground with the toe of his trainer.

"Liam was going to tell you something on the day he died," he says. "Something he wanted you to know."

I hardly dare to breathe, hardly dare believe what I've just heard. Tyler must be telling the truth. I haven't mentioned this to anyone but Gran.

"Go on then – tell me," I challenge.

"Amber?" Simon's voice cuts through the air. I look over my shoulder. My stomach drops as he starts walking our way. "What are you doing out here?" he asks. "I've been searching everywhere for you. There are loads of people—" Simon's eyes lock on to Tyler. "What are you doing here?"

I've never seen Simon look so angry. "You lay one hand on Amber and—" For a horrible moment I think he's going to try to deck Tyler and I put myself in-between them, face to Simon, back to Tyler.

"It's OK, Simon," I say, holding up both hands.

"It is not OK." He speaks to Tyler over the top of my head. "Leave her alone or I'll call the police and tell them everything."

"It's all right mate, I'm going."

I feel pressure against the back pocket of my jeans and I know Tyler's put something there. I turn to look at him but he's already jogging off along the side of the building.

Simon takes a step to follow him but I hold him back. "Let him go," I say. I slip my hand into my jeans pocket and my fingers touch a small piece of paper. I don't take it out.

"You promised me you wouldn't see him," Simon says, his aggression now turned full force on me.

"I didn't plan to see him. I didn't know he was going to be here."

"So what was he doing?" Simon's blocking the path between me and the car park.

"He's a member of the running club. He's got as much right to be here as I have. But he came to tell me he's turned himself into the police and handed over the names of all the others." Simon stares at me in disbelief.

"And I suppose you believe him." Simon says

it with such venom that it knocks the wind out of me. "Don't be taken in," he says. "Don't fall for it, Amber, please."

"For what?" I say coolly.

"For Tyler's lies."

Tyler's bruised body is raw in my memory. I look over my shoulder into the darkness.

I don't think he's lying.

CHAPTER 23

Gran buys about a hundred copies of the local paper. There's a photo of me and a big write-up on the second page along with all the information for organ donation. Gran says I should be pleased about the publicity and I guess I am – it all helps. But the article makes out like I'm some brave, amazing kind of person, a good example for other young people, apparently. I'm not brave or amazing. I'm a coward. I didn't have the courage to speak out about Declan. Tyler did.

I sit at the kitchen table, stare at the article then slam the paper shut. What's the point in all this anyway? It's not going to bring Liam back. It may not even save Jeremy. I thought doing this would help, but now it's come to it, I know it's not enough. I still haven't made it up to the Levines or Liam and, until

I do, I'll never make peace with myself. I finger the slip of paper that Tyler pressed into my back pocket. His phone number.

Mum comes and sits opposite me and pushes a cup of coffee in my direction. She stretches her hand towards me and thumbs away a tear from my face. I lean back out of her reach.

"I've just checked the number of new donors from your campaign," she says quietly. "Three hundred and sixty five – that's one for each day of the year. Fantastic, isn't it?"

I shrug and Mum takes my hand. It is so unexpected, I almost pull it away, but she's gripping tight.

"What you have done is very special," she says. "And very brave. You're braver than your dad and me – you know that don't you?"

Her words find a spot in my brain that's been ignored for a while. My resistance fades a little.

"And it's made me think," she says. "I've had a chat to Siân and she's going to put me on to someone who's going to help me – you know – with my drinking." Mum bites her bottom lip, her eyes examining mine for a reaction. I let the words settle. Perhaps I frown as I try to work out exactly what she's saying.

"I've been a terrible mum. I know that. Grief makes you do stupid things– makes *us* do stupid things. You, me, Dad. Look at us! Then you stand up on that stage and talk to all those people about what is important in life and you tell them your story. That can't have been easy for you and it was an inspiration. You've done something to make life better again. Now I have to do the same. It's not going to be easy for me either, and I may get worse before I get better, but I'm going to try."

Mum has tangled her fingers with mine. Behind the fragile face, I see the old mum looking at me, a steely determination in her eyes. I could tell her that nothing we do will make life better again, that none of it is worth it, but that wouldn't be fair. I don't believe she's got it in her to kick the booze, but I'm not going to put her off trying.

"Amber?"

I shake myself out of my thoughts. "That's brilliant, Mum."

"I'll need your help. I know it's a lot to ask." She's pulling and crunching my fingers between hers. Demanding.

I nod and try to smile while despair drains my last drop energy. Some part of me feels responsible for Mum's drinking. My failure to talk to Liam and find out what was happening; taking his stone; Liam having a genetic heart defect and not me. If anything I did contributed to Liam's death then it also contributed to Mum becoming an alcoholic. I want to help her, but I don't want it to be my fault if she doesn't get better. I don't know if I can deal with that. I fight the urge to disentangle my hand from hers. It's going to be tough for her. The dark shadows under her eyes remind me of Tyler's beaten-up face. Am I somehow responsible for that too?

The door opens and Dad comes into the kitchen, dropping his holdall as he takes in the scene in front of him: Mum and me holding hands across the table. I wait for him to go into the other room, but he doesn't. He pulls up a third chair.

"I've just been talking to Siân," he says.

"You as well?" I ask. I can't quite keep the sarcasm out of my voice.

"She's had a message from Dr Levine."

Mum smiles. "Three hundred and sixty five new donors. Isn't that marvellous."

Dad nods slowly. Then the nod turns to a shake. "It's Jeremy," he says. "I'm afraid he's not winning."

I can tell Dad is trying to tell me kindly. He adds his hands into the middle and I look at him, waiting for more. "His condition has deteriorated. He's being transferred. But he wanted you to know that he is very grateful for what you've done. They all are. Dr Levine said I must tell you that."

I stare helplessly at our three pairs of hands in the middle of the table.

"He can't die," I say. "I promised . . . he can't. . ."

"He's still alive," says Mum. "You mustn't give up hope yet – none of us must give up hope."

"Mum's right," says Dad.

"But it's all my fault. Everything is my fault."

"Of course it's not your fault," says Dad. "What are you talking about?"

"It's me. Don't you see? I'm a disaster." I wrench my hands away and use them to cover my face, screwing my eyes tight shut beneath my fingers. "I can't do anything right. I can't even win a stupid race."

Dad kneels on the floor beside me. I can feel his breath close to me. He takes me in his arms and I don't resist. "Is that really what you think?" he says. "Never, ever think that. None of this is your fault."

"You're wrong. You don't know anything."

"I suppose you're right about that. I don't know much, but I do know this — you are not to blame. If anyone is to blame for all this, it's me." He folds his arms around me and my body collapses against his. He holds me so tightly, he squeezes the breath out of me. "I didn't know how hard this would be," he says. "No one prepares you for losing a child." He takes some great gasping breaths. "I've said and done some terrible things. I know I have. I've been busy trying to survive, but I haven't been surviving — not really — I've just been . . . I don't know . . . hiding." He pushes me away a little, looking at me and then Mum. "I've been a terrible father and a terrible husband."

Mum nods very slightly, her mouth tight.

"I should've realized, should've listened," he says, pressing me closer to him again. "Instead I've made a complete mess of everything and I'm sorry, I'm so sorry." He holds me steady as a rock. "I'm so, so sorry."

"I wanted to win for you but I couldn't," I sob into his shirt. "I wanted Mum to get better. I didn't mean to get into trouble or for Gran to have a heart attack or for Granddad to get cancer and die. I should've talked to Liam before. I should've known

there was something wrong. I should never have. . ."
I stop myself before mentioning the stone. I still
don't have the courage to tell them that.

My chin finds a place to rest on Dad's chest. I
breathe in his smell, feel his warmth. Dad is hugging
me. For the first time since Liam died, Dad is
hugging me. And he's sobbing. And Mum too.

And that's how Gran finds us, clinging to each
other for dear life.

CHAPTER 24

It's kind of strange getting to know your parents again. They're a different Mum and Dad to the ones I knew before. We've got a lot of learning to do – there's no instant fix for a year of damage. It's my campaign that holds us together. Something outside of us that we can all get behind. Jeremy is still hanging in there, though his circulation is now controlled by some machine outside his body.

It makes me stronger, knowing how he's fighting. That's maybe what has brought me here, to see Tyler. I haven't told anyone what I'm doing and I've no idea if it is the right thing. All I know is I have to do it.

My own heart gives an extra beat as I see his car approaching. I know he's seen me. He parks and I walk towards him. He leans over and opens the passenger door, the effort, apparently, making him wince with pain. He's expecting me to get in, but I stand by the open door, cautious. Simon's managed to sow enough doubt to stop me taking any unnecessary chances: this will be done on my terms.

"It's all right. I promise nothing will happen," he says.

"You promised stuff before. Why should I believe you now?"

Tyler shakes his head. He's in an awkward position, diagonally across the passenger seat and cranking his neck up so he can see my face through the open door. That gives me an advantage.

"Things have changed," he says. "They've got Declan banged up. He's got a list of previous that'd stretch half way to Russia." He pushes himself back up to the sitting position and stares straight forward through the windscreen.

I suppose that's supposed to make me feel better, but I still have no proof that Tyler is telling the truth.

"Give me the car keys," I say.

Tyler shrugs, pulls them out of the ignition and throws them on to the passenger seat. I get in the car and shut the door.

"I should've told the police right at the start," I say. "I was a coward."

"No, you weren't. Declan doesn't make idle threats – you were right to be scared."

"He said he wouldn't touch you if I kept my mouth shut. I did keep my mouth shut and look what he did."

Tyler's damaged body, up close, is a sickly mess of purples and yellows. It's healing, but it must have been bad.

"I'm glad you didn't go to the police," he says. "If you'd grassed on me, I wouldn't have had the chance to do it myself. I needed to make that decision. I needed to show Declan he couldn't control me for ever. People like Declan pick on people like us; scoop us up when we're at rock bottom and then do what they want with us. There was never going to be a way out. Not until I broke the deal."

"So what changed?"

"You."

The intensity is back in Tyler's eyes.

"I want to give you this," he says. He seems uneasy.

He puts a crumpled piece of paper on to my lap. It's not what I was hoping for. I recognize it immediately. It's an organ donor registration form. It looks as though it's been screwed up in his pocket for a month. I smooth it out then stare down at it. The form is completely blank apart from Tyler's name.

"Is this supposed to be funny?" I ask.

Tyler's face darkens. "I thought you could fill it in for me."

"Fill it in yourself. It's your body."

Tyler stares at his hands and takes a deep breath.

"I can't."

"It's not that hard."

"I can't."

I give an exasperated sigh. I'm fed up with Tyler playing games with me.

"I can't read or write, OK? I'm dyslexic or whatever they call it. Like my dad. Kelly too, but she's not as bad." He's hunched in on himself now. Avoiding my gaze.

I try to rearrange what I know about Tyler. "But you and Liam were always working on some project or other. I thought – I mean I thought you were really clever. "

"I am clever. I just can't read and write. It's different."

"I'm sorry, I didn't mean it like that." I feel terrible now. "You should've told me before."

"Like I want everyone to know?"

I think back to Tyler at school. I know he was always in trouble and I remember Kelly calling him a dumb-arse, but that's what most people call their brothers. He's tapping the steering wheel fast with both his hands. Like a time bomb counting down.

"You've no idea what it's like. Being in the classroom day after day. Struggling to work out the words, fighting to put anything on paper. It's shit, I'm telling you. I would have been chucked out long before if it hadn't been for Liam being my school mentor. He helped with my work and he got me into running – he said it would get rid of my excess energy so I'd get less angry. He was the only person who understood– the only one who helped. He made life bearable and then he died."

The finality of it all fills the silence.

I'm angry at myself and stunned at how little I know about Tyler; amazed at the secrets people manage to keep.

"Just give me my keys and I'll go," says Tyler. "This was a mistake."

I ram the keys firmly in my pocket. I'm not ready for him to go yet.

"Is that what Liam was going to tell me – on the day he died?" I ask. "Is that why he was shutting me out so much – to protect you, because you didn't want people to know?"

Tyler manages a small smile. "In a way, yes. There's a bit more to it than that."

I wait for the *bit more*, but Tyler covers his face with his hands and the silence stretches and stretches. Finally he puts his hands on his lap and turns to me. "If I tell you everything, you promise you won't judge me?"

"I'm not promising anything, but I'll try."

"And not here. This isn't the right place."

I weigh up my options, take his keys from my pocket and hand them to him. He switches on the engine, puts the car into gear and we start to drive. For all I know he could be driving me straight back into trouble.

The cemetery is open at this time of day and we stroll in. We don't go to Liam's grave but sit on a wooden seat. There's no one else around. Tyler fiddles and fiddles with his fingers, his nails bitten to pieces. I keep thinking he's going to start talking, but then he doesn't.

I force myself to be patient.

"I've moved back in with Sonia and Kelly," he says, eventually.

"Oh – right." This doesn't seem such a big deal.

Tyler shrinks into himself, wrapping his arms around his front. "The police must have got information from someone. They came looking for me. When I told Declan, he lost it; beat me up; cracked two of my ribs. I had to call Kelly. Sonia made me go to the hospital. There were more questions, of course. I decided to tell the police everything. Sonia said she knew someone would beat some sense into me one day and I suppose she was right." He allows himself a stiff smile. "She's a nice lady, she's looked after me. But most of all, I didn't want Declan to get to you."

"Thank you," I whisper. I don't know what else to say.

"All those things you said about Declan – you were right."

319

I shake my head. I'm not sure if I feel sorry for Tyler or plain frustrated. "I can't understand what you were doing hanging out with him in the first place? Anyone could see he was trouble."

"You see what you want to see. He was nice to me in the beginning. I liked the fact he was from out of town; that he didn't know anything about me or Liam or what happened. He introduced me to his mates. They were friendly. It gave me something else to think about. Dad was in prison, I'd been thrown out of school, Sonia more or less kicked me out of home. I didn't have any money, anywhere to go, and I was lonely."

The leaves on the trees are just beginning change colour. I notice this as I listen to Tyler, as I try to absorb the information he's giving me.

"So you were telling the truth – about Liam never knowing him?"

"Yes. I didn't meet Declan 'til weeks after Liam had died." His eyes meet mine and I know he isn't lying. And I'm so grateful. He rubs the palms of his hands up and down his thighs, the material of his jeans rucking up under the pressure.

"I started doing stuff with them – you know, stealing – small first, then bigger. Declan was clever. He kind of sucked us all in. Things felt good."

I remember Simon using those exact words. Sucked in.

"Didn't it worry you, doing all this *stuff*?"

Tyler's eyes are everywhere as he speaks. "I was brought up on stolen goods. I got a buzz when I was with Declan. And I was good at it. That's what Declan told me; I knew the area and I was fast – he liked that – the fact that I could run fast. It felt good to be appreciated, good to be needed. Declan gave a reason to wake up in the morning. He looked after me."

This is not what I want to hear, not what I want to believe.

Suddenly Tyler flops forward as if the fight has gone out of him.

"Yeah, of course it worried me," he says gruffly. "Somewhere deep down. But you don't always think about who you're hurting, do you? I didn't much care about anyone else, I was in it for me."

"So what changed?"

Tyler turns his head to look at me. "I wasn't playing by the rules. Declan told me if I didn't keep my side of the bargain, I was out. He said he wasn't a free meal ticket. That's when he started hassling me."

"What rules? What do you mean 'out'?"

"Declan takes care of me, I take care of Declan. Or else I'm out of his cosy little gang, out of his inner circle, out of the caravan." Tyler's heel bounces up and down on the ground.

"But I thought it was your aunt's caravan. Declan couldn't throw you out of that." Tyler gives me a miserable look. "It wasn't your aunt's?"

He shakes his head. "I relied on Declan for everything. I couldn't survive without him – or that's what he told me. It was payback time and Declan was calling in the favours."

"What did he want from you?"

Tyler thrusts his hands into his pockets and stands up in one swift movement. He walks away about five steps and then turns round and comes back to the seat. The story so far hasn't been easy to listen to and I get the feeling it's about to get a whole lot worse. I can see he's struggling to find the words.

"Declan had this deal going about girls. What was ours was his. He expected us to provide him with – you know. . ."

I struggle to fill in the gap. Does he mean what I think he means?

"Like Joel and Becky. Becky was Joel's girlfriend and that gave Declan the right to be with her whenever he wanted. It was part of the deal. That's how it worked."

"But that's. . .." I'm speechless again. I think back to Joel and Becky and now I see it all. "But I thought Becky liked Declan. She seemed willing enough. Encouraged him, even."

"Yeah – she did. She'd do anything for him and he had no respect for her whatsoever. None. He was bored with her. He was ready for something new and I was supposed to provide it. The trouble is, I didn't have a girlfriend. And that didn't suit Declan one bit. No girlfriend equalled no money, no drugs, nowhere to live. I needed a girlfriend – for Declan."

I try to make sense of what he's telling me. "Let me get this right. Are you saying that if I was your girlfriend, Declan would expect me to sleep with him whenever he wanted and you'd have to be OK with that? Is that what you're saying?" I'm leaning forward so my face is close to Tyler's. I need to be sure there's no misunderstanding.

Tyler nods.

I sit back, stunned. "Why me? What about Kelly's mates – I'm sure a few of them would've been happy to oblige?"

"I didn't want to get Kelly or Sonia involved."

"But it was fine to get me involved?" I stand up. I'm not hanging around here listening to this. Simon was right. I should stay away from Tyler.

He grabs my wrist and holds it. "Please wait," he says. "You said you wouldn't judge me. Let me finish at least."

He lets go of me, making it clear I'm free to leave if I want to. For some reason I sit down again.

"Your family treated me like shit after Liam died. I saw the way you looked at me when I left the hospital that day. You could have stuck up for me, but you didn't. You let your dad spread all those rumours. I'd never have done anything to hurt Liam. It was you who stole his stone on the day he died and some warped part of my brain wanted to make you pay."

I shake my head and laugh in disbelief. "So you thought you'd set me up with Declan? To make me pay?"

"I'd been wanting to contact you for a while. It was time we put a few things straight. The anniversary of Liam's death was coming up and it seemed like a good time."

"Terrific time," I say sarcastically.

"Then Declan started putting the pressure on me and I just thought – why not?"

I look away, trying to distance myself, but this is me he's talking about.

"So you got Kelly to invite me to her party?"

He gives a small shrug. "Didn't think I'd have much chance of getting you to see me otherwise."

"What would've happened if I'd been busy – if I hadn't gone to the party?"

"But you did go."

"But if I hadn't."

"I don't know. I'd have found a way. That's life, isn't it?"

"Is it?" I stare out across the cemetery. I suppose it all comes to this in the end. A hole in the ground.

Tyler gives a deep sigh. "Thing is, it didn't work out like I expected."

"I'm so sorry." I can't keep the sarcasm out of my voice. "I suppose I wasn't willing enough as far as Declan was concerned."

"No, I don't mean that." He turns to face me now, his eyes holding mine. "I mean on the night of the party. Nothing had prepared me for seeing you again. When you turned round – it was like looking at Liam. Everything came flooding back. And you seemed so pleased to see me. I should've taken you straight home. I never planned for us to end up here, at Liam's grave. And I didn't intend for you to stay at the caravan. I thought it would all be simple – but it got complicated."

"Complicated!" I could bloody strangle him. I sit on my hands.

"I didn't realize, until that night, how badly Liam's death had affected you."

"He was my brother! How did you think it was going to affect me?"

He scratches his fingers backwards and forwards through his hair. "That's the thing. I didn't think. I was too cut up by my own sadness, my own anger – that and bombed out on drugs. I wasn't thinking straight. I didn't expect you to like me. I didn't know how being with you would make me feel. By the time I realized I'd got it all wrong, it was too late. You have to believe me. I never meant for you to get involved in all the bad stuff."

"That's crap. You introduced me to Declan, brought me back to the caravan, broke into my house and persuaded me to *help* you and now you're telling me you didn't mean for me to get me involved. Do you think I'm stupid?"

Tyler hangs his head between his knees. "I couldn't see another way. I was trying to buy time. You weren't making things easy for Declan and that upset him – and made him all the more determined. Breaking into your house was Declan's idea, not mine."

"I don't care whose *idea* it was; you didn't have to go along with it."

"At least by being there I thought I could protect you." He laughs a hopeless, sad laugh. "I should've known better. Declan knew too much and he'd worked out he could play one of us off against the other. That gave him added power. He told me what he'd do to you if I didn't co-operate. He'd already been threatening me. Threatening you just gave him added power."

I start to get it – or I think I do. "How do you mean *he knew too much?*"

"You remember the night I took you home after we'd all been together in the caravan?" Tyler looks at me and then stares into the distance. "Declan followed us. I suspected something at the time, more a hunch than anything else, but it turned out I was right. I was a mess that night. I could see what I was dragging you into and I didn't know how to stop it." He clasps and unclasps his hands. "I felt guilty and I was scared – for both of us. I needed to think things through. After I left you I came here."

"To the cemetery?"

Tyler nods. "I went to Liam's grave. I needed to talk to him. I never thought Declan would still be tailing me. I don't know how he managed to get so close without me noticing. As I said, I was a mess. Then Declan overheard every word I said."

For a moment, I wonder why Tyler would talk out loud to a dead person. Then I think of the times that I've done the same; talking to Liam in the empty air, hoping I might get an answer.

"As I got up to leave, Declan appeared. He knew everything now. And that made things a hundred times worse. And he thought it would be helpful if he looked after Liam's stone."

My head is spinning. Tyler is talking in riddles.

"I should have told you straight after Liam died. I would have done if I'd known what I know now."

"What should you have told me?"

"What Liam was going to tell you on the day he died." Tyler examines my face as if he's expecting me to say something. "You really have no idea, do you?" His words make me feel useless and inadequate. I wait. A softness comes over his face, a wisp of a smile. "Liam and me. We loved each other."

For a moment, the world stands still. I turn myself away from Tyler to hide the blush that's burning in my face and neck. In my head, I'm trying to rewrite the last three years, to reel through everything I know about Liam and Tyler and me. The hours they spent locked up in Liam's room. The time they spent training together. Tyler and my brother. Why hadn't Liam told me? I think of the way Tyler held me on Liam's bed, of how he told me I was like my brother.

"You should've said something," I say. "You should've. . ."

"I couldn't. That's what I'm trying to explain to you. If I was going to keep my deal with Declan, I had to pretend to be straight – I *had* to!"

I cover my hand with my mouth as the whole tangled picture begins to unravel in front of me. I feel so stupid for not knowing. I think of the times Tyler and me were together and how awful it must have been for him – pretending. I want to apologize to him, but I don't know what to say.

"Why did Liam hide it from me?" I say. "What did he think; that I'd disapprove or something? This is the twenty-first century. Being gay is not a big deal. I was his sister!" I try to hold back the tide of resentment, the sense of betrayal. "I always thought we were close," I whisper.

Tyler puts his hand on my shoulder. "He *was* going to tell you. He knew he was pushing you away and he hated that as much as you did. He didn't want to hide anything from you, but he was terrified of your dad finding out. Like cripplingly terrified."

"I wouldn't have said anything. Not if he told me not to."

"Not on purpose, but it was an added risk – a risk he wasn't ready to take."

I think about how Dad would've reacted and I know Liam was right. Mum would've been fine, Gran probably would have celebrated, but Dad would've freaked. I think of the hurt it would have caused Liam and Tyler and I understand Liam's terror.

"I'm sorry," Tyler says. "I don't ever expect you to forgive me, but I want you to know I'm sorry."

"Please, please don't be sorry for loving Liam."

"That's not what I mean. I could never be sorry for loving Liam. I'll never meet anyone like him again." He blows out a long, whistling breath, trying to control his emotions. "But I'm sorry about everything else. I wish I could undo what's happened. Liam would've wanted me to take care of you and, instead, look what I've done!" He shakes his head and I almost laugh at the irony of it all. "That's why I needed to see you today. I had to try to explain. And I had to give you this."

Tyler presses something into my hand. It's cold and hard. I open my fingers and stare down at the stone.

"You got it back for me." My eyes swim with tears.

"I promised I would. I wasn't going to let Declan have it, even if it killed me – which it nearly did."

I have to frame my next question carefully. "Tell me honestly, do you think Liam would've survived if he'd been wearing his stone?"

Tyler's face darkens. "I shouldn't have said what I

said earlier. I didn't mean it."

"It's haunted me every day," I say, staring down at the stone in my hands, "that maybe I had something to do with his death – that maybe this stone really is lucky."

Tyler leans back and tips his head towards the sky. "Let me tell you about how he died."

"I know how he died," I say miserably.

"No, you don't. Not the whole story. I haven't told anyone." Tyler takes both my hands, the stone cupped between them. "We'd talked about you in the car and he told me he was going to tell you about us. I was pleased. He said he felt a lot better now he'd made the decision. He was in a hyper-good mood. We started racing. Crazy racing. Laughing. We were pushing each other faster and faster; it was always competitive, both of us wanting to win. Then he said he wasn't feeling good. I thought he was messing around. 'One last race,' I said. I forced him. I made him race me. I was winning. I was laughing. Then he just kind of crumpled and I still laughed and I hugged him and then I realized something was wrong. It was the things he was saying – as if he knew he was going to die. I shouted for help. This bloke tried mouth to mouth and kept thumping Liam's chest . . . the ambulance arrived. There were moments when I thought there was still hope. I blamed myself for pushing him too hard, I blamed you for taking his stone, I blamed your dad, the world, anything. But this heart problem existed before he found his stone, before you were born, before he met me. It was in his genes. There's nothing anyone could do about that."

Tyler's matter-of-fact tone can't hide the emotions inside. He lets go of my hands. Every angle of his body, every muscle, every joint spells out his agony.

"Still," he says with a small smile, "I wish it hadn't happened when he was out running with me."

My mind slips back to the hospital, to Dad screaming at Tyler. I can't bear to think about it knowing what I know now.

"I wish it hadn't happened on the day I took his stone," I say.

He gives my shoulder a reassuring squeeze. "You only borrowed it. You were going to give it back."

I steeple my fingers. "Yes, I was, but I never got

the chance. And I'm glad it's you that was with him. He loved you. More than anything, he would've wanted you with him when he died."

I sense a small giving of the tension in Tyler's body. "He loved you too," he says.

We sit for a space of minutes without talking.

I put my head on Tyler's shoulder. Suddenly the fact that Liam loved him is very, very important. Being close to Tyler makes me feel close to Liam again. I don't feel shut out any more. But I'm still struggling to fit everything into place.

"That night at Kelly's, did you steal my keys and phone?"

"Yes. Spur of the moment – it wasn't planned."

"But then you had the excuse to come to my house?"

"Again, not planned exactly. But I was desperate to see Liam's room again."

"God, Tyler, you don't make things easy, do you?"

I turn Liam's stone over in my hand. It's not cold now.

"I think you should keep it," I say holding it out to him. "Liam would want you to have it."

Tyler ignores me. His forehead is gathered into a deep frown.

I take the stone between my thumb and forefinger and hold it up, angling it so the sun shines straight through the hole in the centre, small flashes of blue glistening in the bright light.

"Maybe Liam had a hand in all this after all," I say. "It may sound crazy, but at least we've got away from Declan and, in some bizarre way, it's got my family back together again."

"Maybe," says Tyler. We both stare up at the stone.

"So what next?" I ask.

"I think we should give it back to Liam, don't you?"

I look at him and smile. I don't know why I hadn't thought of it myself. I let the stone drop back into the palm of my hand.

"So," he says, "are you ready?"

He stands up and takes me by the hand and we walk in silence towards Liam's grave. We both kneel and Tyler takes a penknife from his pocket and cuts away a small square of grass. We dig into the earth beneath until we have made a deep hole.

I bring the stone to my lips and give it a kiss then hand it to Tyler. He does the same. Then we both take hold of the thin leather lanyard and lower the stone into the hole. I'm not sure either of us breathes. We pack the earth in over the top of it and press down hard. You'd hardly know the ground had been touched.

Tyler gives a small sniff and says, "He'll be happy now."

I close my eyes. An intense peacefulness fills my whole body. We kneel, in silence, for a few more moments and then we both stand. This time when Tyler's arms go round me it feels perfect. In some strange way I feel happier than I've felt since. . . I can't even remember the last time I felt happy.

"Do you think he's watching us?" I say.

"No. I think he's had enough of us. You and me – we've got to sort ourselves out and try to make something of the rest of our lives."

He starts to laugh. Is it OK to laugh? Is it?

"Come on," he says. "I'll race you to the car."

By the time we arrive, breathless, we're both laughing.

CHAPTER 25

It's hard to believe another year has passed. The final race of the season is here. I've been training hard; not because Dad has made me but because I want to; I have my own timetable and my own agenda.

Jeremy's there, standing with Simon. They watch as I warm up with my friends.

"Coming to join us?" I shout over to them.

"Are you joking?" Simon says. "Jeremy and me — we'd thrash you all, no question."

Jeremy looks so frail, wrapped up even though it's warm. But he's alive, his transplant was successful and life is getting back to normal.

Dad's chatting to the other parents and paying no attention to me. I love him for that. But when our race is called, he comes over and whispers in my ear, "Just enjoy it. But don't let them get you on the final sprint."

"Shut up," I say, laughing and he strides off with a huge grin on his face. If I'm totally honest, I think there's still a hint of tension in his shoulders, a tiny breath of expectation. I would like to win for him — just once.

I run a good race but they do get me in the final sprint. I come fourth and I'm happy enough. No trophy or medal, but that's life.

After all the racing is over, we head to the hall for prize-giving. It'll be a long one as it covers all the running club events, including athletics, for all ages. Jeremy's been invited to give out the prizes — on account of his exceptional good looks, he tells me. Tyler wins the men's trophy and even Mum and Dad look happy. I asked Siân if she could help put things right between Tyler and Dad. I thought it would help Tyler but I think it helped Dad more. I can't help wondering if Mum and Dad knew about Tyler and Liam. One day, maybe I'll ask them. I reckon they'd be fine with it. Simon goes up to Tyler, shakes his hand and slaps him on the back. I never thought I'd see the day that those two became good mates — though it took a bit of time.

At the end of the formal prize-giving, the

president stands up to give his end of season speech. I hope he keeps it short. I let my mind wander. I'm supposed to have decided what movie to go and see with Simon this evening.

". . .and we have one last trophy this year, the Liam Neville cup for the most valued member of the club."

At Liam's name, my attention jolts back to the president. I look at Dad and he shrugs as if he knows nothing about it, but he's grinning.

"This year, I am sure you'll all agree that the trophy should be awarded to Amber. Thanks to her amazing campaign, more than a thousand new organ donors have signed up. It is also a fitting tribute to her brother Liam, who was one of the most talented runners this club has ever had."

I'm half crying, half smiling as I go to the front. The president shakes my hand, and Jeremy hands over a small silver cup. Hanging from one of the handles by a chain is a tiny stone with a hole in it.

"Did you have something to do with this?" I whisper.

"No – nothing to do with me." He nods towards the back of the room. "You might want to speak to Tyler."

I make my way to the back, people congratulating me on the way.

"So?" I say, holding up the cup.

He doesn't have to say anything, I can tell by his face.

"You didn't steal it did you?"

He raises both eyebrows in a *wouldn't you like to know* kind of way. We both laugh.

Dad hurries over and puts one arm around Tyler and one around me.

I can see Mum and Gran chatting to Dr Levine — Chris, as I now call him. Mum's only had one relapse into drinking and that was when Dad spilled the beans about his girlfriend. It's all over now and it wasn't as if Mum didn't know. Since then, she's been clean for seven months, three weeks and two days. But who's counting?!

Dad takes the cup from me and examines it closely.

"This is a real trophy," he says. "No one could've fought harder for it and no one deserves it more. One for the cabinet, I think."

I touch the little stone.

A siren wails in the distance.

Someone else's flash of blue.

For more information about
organ donation, visit
www.organdonation.nhs.uk

ACKNOWLEDGEMENTS

It is always a bonus when experts are happy to share their knowledge and experience over a cup of coffee or two! In this regard, I am indebted to Tony Walker for his extensive insights into restorative justice and for reading and commenting on large sections of my manuscript; to Alison Gadd for her expertise in the safeguarding of children and for providing me with information on the detention, treatment and questioning of persons by police officers; to Anna Tylor for her astounding breadth of knowledge over a huge range of social issues, her lifelong friendship and for making me laugh and cry in equal measure and to Eva Hamilton who, through her work with Key4Life, provided a source of inspiration for the novel. If I have misrepresented any of their information in the book, then it is entirely my fault!

I would also like to recognize the extraordinary dedication, skill and care of all the staff in the heart transplant team at Papworth Hospital. We, like so many families, will never be able to thank them enough.

And last, but absolutely not least, a huge thank you to the team at Scholastic, to my editor, Helen Thomas and my agent, Juliet Mushens. Between them they keep the business of writing interesting, inspiring and fun.

Maria is a speech therapist and teacher and has spent much of her life working with students with learning difficulties. She read Speech Sciences at UCL and, more recently, graduated from Bath Spa University with an MA in Writing for Young People. She has four daughters, a brave husband and a young dog. Her biggest challenge is sitting still for long enough to write a book. *A Flash of Blue* is her second novel.

@FarrerMaria
www.mariafarrer.com

BRO KEN
STRI NGS

Love, ambition
or secrets –
which will break
you first?

Maria
Farrer

Jess has one chance to win the music scholarship
that will change her life. When she fails, she believes
she's lost everything, including her only shot with
the boy she loves.

But then Jess gets an offer to start again from
someone she didn't even know existed.

It's a second chance, but it comes at a price.
Threatened by shadows from the past, Jess realizes
she's fighting for more than just her own dreams. . .